THE
CONFLUENCE

Gary Hope

"The Confluence," by Gary Hope. ISBN 978-1-62137-995-9 (softcover).

Published 2017 by Virtualbookworm.com Publishing Inc., P.O. Box 9949, College Station, TX , 77842, US.

Dedication

To: The Liverpudlian and Robesonian boys...thanks for the dreams

Ed, John, Ernest, Michael, John, et al...thanks for the inspiration

SC-H, KCH, SCH, EAH, DTH, CER...thanks for your love

George, Amanda; Abbey, Juliette; Mark, Niamh and Claire...thanks

GRH...what are you going to do with your one wild and precious life?

For all of you who have been lucky enough to see and experience the Confluence ... keep the dream alive.

Other works of fiction
by the author are:

"It's Too Late To Die Young Now"

"Abbey"

"The Girl From Tir-na-nOg"

Contents

1

THE AIR WAS SO HEAVY that I could sense the rain, and even though it hadn't actually started, I could feel it. But even if it did rain, I still felt good. I'd just come out of Panera Bread where I had a cup of dark roast coffee and a blueberry bagel with peanut butter. I was happy, full, and had nothing on my mind as I walked out the door towards my car. Before I could step off the curb, however, a homeless man, black, about sixty years old with graying hair and the looks of a person who'd led a hard life, came up to me and said, "Excuse me, sir. I'm homeless and hungry and was hoping you had some spare change so I could get something to eat. But I understand if you don't."

I generally just say "No." Or "Sorry" and walk away but, there was something about him that made me stop. What? I don't know, but I stopped and looked in my wallet only to find three twenty dollar bills. I looked back at him and said, "I only have a twenty and I need that for lunch today. I'm sorry." It was sort of the truth and sort of a lie—either way it made me feel bad. He thanked me and turned to walk away and I continued on to my car. When I sat down in my car, before starting the engine, I couldn't stop thinking of the homeless guy...there was something about him. I decided to go back into Panera and get change for a twenty dollar bill and give the guy five bucks.

I walked back towards the store and saw the homeless man about twenty yards away, looking up at the cloudy sky. I went back in and got change, which baffled the clerk inside Panera to no end. She couldn't understand why I wanted change for a twenty while not buying anything. She actually called the assistant manager,

Ida, over to okay giving me change. When I finally did get the money changed and walked back outside, a light rain had begun.

I walked over to the man, handed him five dollars and said, "I hope this helps a little. Try to stay dry and have a great day."

He looked back at me and replied, "Thanks, Jerry, I really appreciate it."

What? He just said my name! How does he know my name? Completely confused, I asked him, "How do you know my name?"

"I know who you are. Thanks again, Jerry." And he turned and walked away. I stood for a moment or two and watched him, trying to decide if I should go after him and demand a better answer or just let it go. I was totally bewildered and confused— how did this stranger know my name? I got back in my car, but couldn't start it; I had to know more about what had just happened. I quickly got out of the car again to go back and talk to this man, but when I started walking back towards Panera and the shopping center, I didn't see him anywhere. I know he didn't go in Panera, or the clothing store next door, because it hadn't opened yet. I looked all around, but he was gone. As I was standing there in the rain trying to understand what had just happened, a car came up behind me and blew the horn, startling me. I was standing in the driveway blocking traffic. I waved an apology and went back to my car, wet and perplexed. I sat there looking around for a few minutes, then drove around the parking lot of the shopping center, but I never saw him.

I drove back towards work wondering how a homeless, black man I'd never seen or met before knew my name. I had no answer. After work I thought of telling my girlfriend about the story, but she was usually a little too concerned with her own thoughts to be very attentive to any musings I might have. So, I did what I usually did and listened to her daily ritual of complaints, annoyances and whining about everything from her crazy boss, her idiotic customers, her parents, her friends, and ultimately the sad and boring affairs of her personal life— meaning me! She is not a happy person. In fact, she's never been a happy person. Knowing all this, you may ask why I'm involved with such a self-absorbed, unpleasant, self-centered woman. Because I'm engaged to her, that's why. Okay, Jerry, next question: Why are you engaged to a self-absorbed, self-centered woman like this? The answer is rather simple-- I'm too lazy to break it off and find someone else. And, my mom says I couldn't find anyone better. Thanks, Mom.

I really think it's because my mother is concerned I'm getting older and my time to present her with grandchildren may be disappearing. I have found it a bit disconcerting lately that my girlfriend and my mother have discussed the possibility of children without even acknowledging my thoughts on the matter, or without asking if I actually want to marry this woman and procreate with her. As if I actually have a choice in the matter. We've been dating for almost three years now, so I guess we should get married. It's the logical, sensible thing to do...right? Does it matter that we really don't like each other? Or that she's never actually told me that she loves me? When I confessed my love to her that first time, which was declared after a passionate night of you-know-what, she returned my admission of love with this statement: "Thanks, Jerry, that's so sweet."

And so, here we are...one of us too lazy to do anything about it; the other too selfish to do anything about it. Both doomed to a life of blah, boredom, indifference, and monotony. All for the sake of procreating to make everyone ELSE happy. The more I understand about my situation, the sadder I get. I'm an adult, but not like a real adult. It's best not to think about it too much though; just accept the inevitable and follow the plan.

I'm an intelligent sort of guy, just not very smart or hard-working when it comes to my future. I have a mid-level management job in a waste disposal company that requires little imagination or fortitude, which fits me very well. My life can be pretty boring, unless I put some effort into it, which I'm not equipped to do at the moment. My mother has quite a nest egg built from my father's savings and then his life insurance when he suddenly died of a heart attack several years ago. I'm pretty sure this is the main appeal I present to my girlfriend turned fiancée. Well, that and my average good looks and less than aggressive professional future.

Before my father died, I had asked Jennifer out on a date and she turned me down flat. She didn't even offer an excuse, she just said, "No." But after dad died and Jennifer's mom found out from my mom (they are in the same Sunday school class) about the substantial life insurance policy, her interest in me suddenly bloomed. Somehow, I kept "running" into Jennifer at various places around town—places I'd never run into her before. Life can be strange that way. One thing led to another and we started the dating process a few years back.

I've never had any long-term girlfriends in my life, so I'm a little inexperienced in that department. But Jennifer is not exactly what I imagined a serious girlfriend would be like. Don't misunderstand, she's nice to look at, but a little uninspiring to talk with and very demanding. She graduated from Salem College with a degree in Early-American Art. When that major didn't offer her many (meaning none) job opportunities, she took a position in the human resources department of a small factory here in Winston-Salem, my hometown. She has an apartment downtown, in the yuppie quarter, and I have a small house in the West End section of Winston. I like my little house, but Jennifer doesn't. She's already making plans and looking around for a more "suitable" location for us to live when the fateful day arrives.

Jennifer's parents are pretty ambivalent about the imminent nuptials of their oldest daughter. Their younger daughter is already married with two kids thereby satisfying their grandparenting instincts. Her mom pretty much ignores me, which is fine, because she's not a nice person, much like her daughter. Jennifer's parents are divorced and she has little to do with her dad, who is quite the character. He's been a golf pro at several country clubs around town his entire life. He could have been a very good one if he could've figured out a way to keep the bottle under par and his libido from double-bogeying. He went to East Carolina University, which is not the best place in the world to attend if drinking might be in your future, but he was a minor star on their golf team. I'm not sure he attended many classes and when I asked him what he majored in at ECU, he said, "I majored in staying out of the Vietnam War." An admirable course of studies during the early 1970's.

Jennifer always refers to her dad in the past tense: "He was fun to be around." Or, "I think I was his favorite." She rarely sees him now, since he doesn't have a lot to offer her except a mimosa or cocktail. And, she's usually older than most of his girlfriends, and not nearly as well-endowed, which hurts her feelings even more. But, I'm digressing...I'm sure Jennifer will make a wonderful wife and excellent mother. I tell myself that each and every day in the hope that I will someday start believing it.

2

ALL OF THE ABOVE is the reason I keep returning to Panera Bread each day, in the unpredictable and vagary chance that I might meet this illusory, homeless man who knew ME, Jerry Dixon McRacken. I make the side trip most days, eat the obligatory bagel and drink the requisite coffee. I even keep a five dollar bill hidden inside my wallet, but alas, I do not see the man anywhere or anytime. It's disappointing, but in a sense, maybe a relief. What would I say to him if I did see him again? What would I expect him to say? But, better an "oops" than a "what if." Don't try to figure everything out at once, Jerry, and remember, it's always too early to quit dreaming.

I've been going to Panera so often that Ida, the assistant manager, the cashiers and even the cooks all know my name now. When I enter, they wave and say, "Hey, Jerry, peanut butter today?" I guess I'm the only non-cream cheese eater they see. I started not to go today because I have to go to a dinner tonight with Jennifer and her so-called best friend, Casey. Normally, a dinner with Jennifer would be pretty bland and uninspiring, but Casey makes it a tad more tolerable. A lot more tolerable if you're into cleavage and long legs...which, obviously, I'm not.

I didn't want to fill up on peanut butter and bagel, but my Panera habit is too much to overcome. However, I run into bad luck when I find that Baptist Hospital has scheduled an off-site meeting for some staff people here and the entire restaurant is filled with these scrub-wearing, young, professional do-gooders. Don't you just hate people like that?

The line is nearly out the door, but I join in and wait my turn. If they'd all just order a bagel, like me, the line would zip right along; but no, they have to order specialty sandwiches, mochas, lattes, and smoothies. The line slowly moves forward and I'm next to order when someone passes through the line behind me. I shuffle forward a little to make space; as I do this woman—I think it's a woman—says, "She's not right for you."

As I'm hearing this the assistant manager, Ida, says, "Good morning, Jerry. Blueberry or cinnamon and raisin today?"

I'm momentarily confused and can't decide whether to answer the bagel question or turn to look at the woman who spoke to me. THINK! I quickly say "blueberry" then turn to look for the woman who spoke. All I see are more people in scrubs standing in line behind me, all talking to each other or texting someone even more important than the friend they're with. Then I notice the door closing and a woman walking outside towards the parking lot.

Then Ida says, "Coffee with that? Jerry?"

I turn and say, "Yes, thanks." And when I look back outside, the woman is gone; I can't see her anywhere. I quickly ask Ida if she saw the woman who passed in line behind me—of course, she has no clue what I'm talking about. There's a very attractive Asian young lady, in scrubs, standing in line behind me talking on her cell phone. I interrupt her conversation and ask if she saw the woman who just passed through and spoke to me. She frowns, while saying "No," and turns away from me. As I get my order, I notice she's off her phone so I ask her again if she happened to notice the woman who passed between us in line. She answers, "What woman?" I hope she's more observant when she's operating on someone's gall bladder.

Ida says something to me about the weather I think, I'm not sure. I take my coffee and bagel and find an open seat near the window. I look at every car that passes, but can't find what I think might be the woman who spoke to me. "She's not right for you." Those are the words I heard as plain as day. I can't eat my bagel. The peanut butter will have to be wasted. The coffee is getting cold. And I can't move.

Jennifer and I meet Casey for dinner at Vincenzo's, which is the best Italian restaurant in town, other than Paul's, of course. Jennifer has the eggplant parmigiana, Casey has veal parmigiana, and I have thoughts running through my mind like you wouldn't believe. Fortunately, I am rarely involved in the conversation, so my thoughts can wander from here to eternity—as the case may be. I can't stop thinking about that statement, "She's not right for you." First, how did this unknown woman know me? Second, who was she referring to? And third, why did she say she's not right for me?

I have no answer for the first two questions, but the third question can be answered, if I'm brave enough. Am I? Instead of eating my dinner, I think too much. I try to convince myself what I heard was just a coincidence—a quirk of fate, an anomaly, an aberration, and a deviation from reality. But no...who am I fooling? I heard what I heard. Then, an epiphany: No reason to stay, is a good reason to go!

By my second glass of Shelton's Riesling and a piece of key lime pie, I'm convinced I have to do something. What? I have no idea, but I know I must do something and I think I'm going to like doing it. I have to remind myself that I cannot fail at being myself. But me being me requires some outside validation for all this thinking. I don't trust myself that much. After dinner, I beg off from any further activities the girls have planned, citing a big day tomorrow. Casey hugs me and gives me a kiss on the cheek; Jennifer shakes my hand and says, "Call me later." We both know that won't happen.

When I get home I call the only person I feel I can be halfway honest with and discuss this turn of events with—my bartender. He's really my cousin, who happens to be a bartender. Either way, he's a good listener and has no problem telling me when he thinks I'm full of crap. Joe is seven years older than me so that gives him the semblance of better judgment and wisdom than his younger cousin. I've decided not to tell him of my chance meeting with the homeless man or the woman in Panera. I want him to listen to me, not ridicule me. So, I just tell him of my doubts about my future with Jennifer. He first says, "You'd better thank your lucky stars you can even find one woman who'd take your sorry butt. Look at you: you're ugly, lazy, broke, and worthless."

If he wasn't my cousin I'd hang up on him, but I think he's only kidding. You are kidding aren't you, Joe? Before I can actually ask him this question he starts laughing. Whew!

"What sort of doubts?" he asks. "Do you think she's banging someone else?"

"No, I don't think that at all."

"Are you banging someone else?"

"Of course I'm not. I wouldn't do that to Jennifer."

He pauses a little, then asks, "You don't love her anymore?"

"Joe, I'm not sure I've ever loved her." I think about that statement a little, then add, "Love is not really the basis of our relationship."

After a suitably long period of silence, he says, "Son, if love is not the basis of your relationship, then you're in the wrong relationship."

"But she's nice and looks pretty good and I can trust her. I think she'll make a great mom, if we have kids. And she has a good job and works hard. I think we're a pretty good fit." I know what Joe is thinking, so I continue my argument: "And listen, if you can have all those things and feel really comfortable with them, then maybe love isn't the most important thing in a relationship."

"Did you hear that horse hockey from Dr. Phil or Oprah? Look, idiot, without LOVE all that other stuff doesn't add up to a hill of string beans! If she doesn't make your heart skip a beat, or make the devil inside you start screaming naughty little thoughts, then all the COMFORTABLE in the world will never be enough."

I know he's right, but instead I reply, "I'm not sure that's right, Joe."

"Well then, you're an idiot and you and her are both doomed to a life of misery, which it seems as though you might enjoy."

"No, I don't want to be miserable, I'm just not sure I'll ever find someone as good as Jennifer is. She's really a good person."

"I'm hanging up," Joe says disgustedly. "Not once during this entire, weird conversation have you told me that you loved her with all your heart. That in itself is grounds to break it off and find someone who sets your loins on fire and makes your heart flutter. Trust me, doofus. Goodnight."

Earlier this morning, walking into Panera, all I wanted was a bagel. I was content, I was fairly happy, my life seemed set, and then some woman walks behind me in line and my entire world changes. Heck, she may have been talking to someone else and I just overheard her. But I know I'll never convince myself of that. I heard her and strangely enough, I think she's right.

3

AFTER DINNER AT VINCENZO'S, Jennifer and Casey decide to go to Katherine's Brasserie for a glass or two of wine and some girl talk. Casey could have any guy in town with her looks and personality, but she's been dating this guy she met at her gym who works for UPS. Jennifer has met this fellow and just doesn't understand the appeal. Whereas Casey is gorgeous, smart, educated, and very successful, this man only attended Forsyth Tech for a year and a half and has been working at UPS ever since dropping out of school. Sure, he's attractive, in a physical sort of way, but as Jennifer sees it—looks aren't everything.

After a glass of Riesling at dinner and now a glass and a half of Merlot (from California no less), Jennifer has the courage to ask her friend what's going on with this guy. Why can't she meet a stable, solid man with a future—like her Jerry? One more sip and she barges ahead, "What's going on with this guy, Eric, from your gym? I know you like him, but really Casey, is there a future with him? I mean, can you really see yourself married to a UPS guy in a brown uniform? You need to start thinking about your future and finding someone solid you can depend on."

Casey knew this conversation would eventually happen. She could sense the disdainful looks Jennifer gave her whenever she talked about Eric. As she sat her glass of wine down, Jennifer asked further, "Why do you keep seeing him? Can you explain it? Is it just the sex?"

Casey takes a deep breath and replies, "Yes, I can totally explain it. He makes me laugh and he sets my heart on fire. He's the first person I want to speak with in the morning and last person I want to see at night. When I close my eyes, I see him. When I dream, I dream of him. When I see me twenty years from now, I see him by my side, making me laugh, making me happy, and making me horny. In fact, I can't imagine ever not seeing him in my life."

Jennifer was not expecting this response. She takes another sip of the dry and bland Merlot and says, "Well, other things are just as important."

Casey looks at her and replies, "Really? Name one."

"What about financial security? Have you ever thought of that? I mean really, a UPS driver?"

Casey's face is a little flushed as she explains, "He's not a full-time driver, Jennifer. He does fill in around holidays to help out, but he generally works on the docks and in the office. And if you must know, he makes over a hundred and ten thousand dollars, plus his pension."

Jennifer's lower lip quivers a little as she tries to comprehend this information. Then she says, "Well, money's not everything! Compatibility is much more important. Having someone you can trust, like I do with Jerry, is definitely the most important thing in a relationship."

Casey smiles and takes a small sip of wine. She knows what's important and she suspects Jennifer does as well, but will never admit it.

This morning, Friday, is good because it's the end of the work week, but bad because it's my last day this week to go back to Panera and try to find either the homeless man or the mystery woman. When I make my way in the parking lot, I don't see any homeless men standing around, which I didn't really expect. I've

12

almost convinced myself now that I half imagined what I heard that day—I'm almost certain of it.

I walk in Panera and see the usual crowd: a group of retirees discussing their ailments and comparing all the medicines they each take. Another group of middle-aged women just coming from their daily yoga and Pilates classes, desperately trying to stay fit and attractive for their hard-working husbands—or boyfriends, or both. Several groups of college-aged kids, all insanely addicted to their I-pads and cell phones, are reading and texting their other friends who aren't as fortunate as they are to be in Panera drinking free coffee and acting millennial.

I glance over the crowd, quite anonymously I might add, and don't see the mystery woman. I order a blueberry bagel with peanut butter and coffee and look out the front window and door, where I don't see the mystery homeless man either. I find me a nice out-of-the-way table and finish eating and get a coffee refill still not seeing the mystery woman. Then I wonder, would I actually recognize her if I did see her again? I only caught a glimpse of her as she walked out the door and into the parking lot. I'm not exactly sure what she looked like. I think she had brown hair—maybe. She wasn't tall, nor was she short; and she wasn't fat. But I'd know her if I saw her again...I'm sure of it. She had that something that's unexplainable, yet very definable. I, however, can't seem to define it. So, I continue looking.

After my second cup of light roasted coffee, I give up and go back to work. Should I talk with Jennifer this weekend? I think I should. But, maybe it'll be better to wait a bit so I can formulate my thoughts and make sure I'm doing the right thing. That, plus I'm a coward and she has a terrible temper.

At our usual dinner date on Friday night, Jennifer surprises me by asking, right out of the blue, "How much money do you actually make?" We've discussed finances before, in general terms, but not specifically how much money we each make. I'm trying to decide three things as she's staring at me: Do I tell her the truth? Why does she want to know? And, if we're going to break up (at some point), do I want her knowing how much, or little, money I make? After a quick deliberation, I decide to lie to her and tell her I make about $65,000. I don't make $65,000, but maybe she'll never know that.

The news of my fabricated earnings seems to depress her a bit, but she brightens up by telling me she has some great news, "Mom and I have decided we should get married in the mountains this fall. With all the leaves turning colors, it'll be beautiful."

I really, really want to say, "Well, I hope you and your mom have a great wedding." But I don't. Instead, she continues babbling about wedding junk, while I'm silently wondering why I should marry a woman who has still never to this day ever told me she actually loves me.

I nod approvingly, but say nothing. Fall is still a few months away, so I have time to squirm out of this if I so desire. After all, I have not officially asked Jennifer to marry me, nor have I bought any engagement ring. Then comes another surprise, Jennifer says, "You're the last thing I think of every night before I go to sleep." Then she leans over and kisses me on the cheek right there in the restaurant. Maybe I've got her all wrong. Maybe she does love me. Maybe Jennifer is the girl for me. Maybe this mystery woman is seriously mistaken. I need to do a lot of thinking.

What was I thinking? I know Jennifer is the right woman for me. Last night, after the HBO movie was over, I took her hand and told her I truly loved her and was looking forward to our marriage. She smiled and said "We're going to be very happy. You make me laugh."

"I make her laugh?" That was an odd thing to say after I told her again that I loved her. Anyway, plans are progressing and tomorrow after work I'm going to look at engagement rings. Jennifer told me the type of ring she wanted, I just need to pick out an appropriate size (meaning one I can afford). The jewelry store is at Reynolda Village, which is great, so I don't have to drive over to the mall and get stuck in all that traffic. At least, I thought it was great until I walked in and saw some prices of rings in the display case.

A very attractive sales lady asked what I was looking for. That is really easy for me, since Jennifer has told me what to buy. In fact, she wrote it down on a piece of paper to give them, so I wouldn't forget and screw it up. The saleswoman asked me if this was to be an engagement ring. I told her it was, that my fiancée had picked it out. She nodded, then looked directly in my eyes and said, "Jerry, she's not the girl for you." And with that explosive statement, she took the piece of paper I'd given her, with the instructions from Jennifer, turned around, and walked into the back storeroom.

I didn't move. I'm desperately trying to remember if I'd told her my name when I came in. I must have told her—how else would she know? As I'm strenuously trying to remember everything I've said since I came in the store, an older man, with a nametag that says Alvin Tostig, comes out from an office and walks over to me. He asks, "Can I help you find something in particular?"

I answer, "The other lady is helping me. She'll be right back."

He quizzically looks at me and asks, "What other lady?"

"The other sales lady, she just went in the back."

He looks towards the back and points that way saying, "You're telling me a lady just went back there?"

"Yes," I said, pointing in that direction.

He suddenly ran around behind the counter, opened up a drawer, and came out with a pistol. He looked at me and said, "If you have a cell phone, run outside and call 911." Then he punched a button on the wall and started walking towards the back room. I followed his instructions and ran outside. I was so flustered and scared that I totally forgot to call 911 for him, but there was no need—two police cars, with lights and sirens flashing, pulled into the parking lot. The first policeman had a gun drawn and yelled at me to put my hands up in the air. I tried to tell him I was just a customer, but he pointed his gun at me and screamed to get my hands in the air. This time I followed his instructions. The second policeman ran past us into the store, while the first policeman kept his eye on me.

After a minute or two, the policeman and the man from the store came outside with us and the policeman asked the man if I was the guy in the store. He said, "Yes, that's the man who tried to rob me."

Before I could say a word, my policeman pulled my arms down and was handcuffing me. All the shoppers and store owners from the surrounding businesses came out to see what was happening and catch a glimpse of the "robber." Me!

I tried to say something, but they told me to shut up. They started asking me if I had any weapons on me, and if I had a partner. During this time, two more police cars came pulling in and people were running and screaming. They still would not allow me to say anything. They searched the store, and when they satisfied themselves that nothing had indeed been stolen, the owner started to settle down a bit. Then they asked me again if I was trying to rob this store alone, or did I have help.

Finally, I was able to speak. I told them exactly what had happened. That his assistant had gone into the back room to check something, then he came out, reached in a drawer, pulled out a gun, and ran into the back room with the woman, while telling me to run outside. They turned and asked the owner to verify that story. He said, "I have no assistant and there was not a woman in the back room. He left this note describing a ring in the back room, that's why I know he was there. He made that up in order to rob me and get away!"

What? I told them again...I was shopping for a ring and his assistant was helping me. She took my note and went into the back room and that's when things got crazy. The man started screaming, "I have no assistant; my brother and I own and operate this store and he's at home now. There is no woman, unless she's his partner trying to rob me."

The store owner then came toward me yelling and pointing his finger at me. The police stopped him and said, "Let's all settle down and we'll figure this out." We each repeated our story several times, including once into a tape recorder. The owner said he has a store camera but doesn't turn it on until he closes the shop for the night. After a couple of hours it was ascertained that nothing was stolen, that no weapon was shown by me, and that I didn't try to make a get-away. Before letting me go home, the policemen took my name and address, got my driver's license information, and then took my picture. As I finally got in my car, the store owner cursed at me and screamed if he ever saw me in his store again, he'd shoot me!

Who in the whole, wide world is ever going to believe this story?

4

I REMEMBER SMOKING a marijuana cigarette once in college...okay, maybe more than once. But that was a long time ago. I can't be having flashbacks from that can I? How else do I explain what just happened to me? I had a conversation with a sales woman, who obviously didn't exist. This woman, who didn't exist, knew my name and also told me that ". . . she's not the girl for you." My more immediate problem is explaining this bizarre event to Jennifer. No...that'll never work. I'll have to explain to her that the jewelry store didn't have what she wanted, and that I'll continue shopping at jewelry stores near the dreaded mall.

I was meeting Jennifer and her mom for dinner at Village Tavern, so I could tell them I'd bought the engagement ring they both wanted for her. Neither of them could understand why I didn't buy the ring they both picked out at the jewelry store in Reynolda Village a few days before. I don't think they truly believed me when I said the ring must have sold, because it wasn't available any longer. I'm pretty sure her mom just thinks I'm cheap. Jennifer probably thinks I'm getting cold feet and trying to delay things. I think I might be going crazy! They finally got over their disappointment with the anticipation of going out to the mall and shopping in several other stores for a different (and probably more expensive) ring.

I need some time alone. I need to try and figure this out. I need a drink—or two. This is the third time someone I've never seen or met before has known my name. And it's getting worse. This last woman was apparently only visible to me. I don't know if some way or another she disappeared, or if I somehow imagined her. Am I losing my mind? If I was a regular church goer I'd call the preacher and have a heart-to-heart talk with him. But I'm not. I want to be, but apparently I'm too lazy to get up Sunday mornings and actually go to church. I can't talk to my cousin Joe—I know him too well and he'd just think I was making it all up for a joke. I need someone who'll listen to me and understand. I need to call a good friend. I need to call Mary.

Mary and I went to grade school and high school together; we lived on the same block and have known each other nearly our entire lives. She was somewhat of a tomboy and was actually a better athlete than I was. She could outrun me and beat me in tennis and ping-pong. And, she was the first girl to see my privates, although we were only six at the time. I can talk to Mary, I can tell her stuff I wouldn't be able to tell anyone else. She'll listen and understand. She doesn't particularly like Jennifer, but she doesn't really know her either. They went to different high schools and were never in the same social groups. Mary was an athlete and very popular. Jennifer was...not.

All through high school and college, Mary would be the one I'd tell about the girls I wanted to date. And, I'm pretty sure that in high school she helped me arrange a few dates by working behind the scenes. We went to different colleges: I stayed home and commuted to UNC-Greensboro and Mary went to Appalachian State University, in Boone. But we stayed in touch and hung out during summers and holidays. Even though she's never discussed it, I've always had the impression Mary is a lesbian. Some things are better left unspoken and someone's private life is their affair—not mine.

All through high school, I thought of Mary as one of the "guys." We hung out together, listened to music, went to concerts and a few ball games—she was one of us. In high school Mary was a tomboy with a tomboy figure--very athletic and not very feminine. Then, during her last couple of years in college, Mary started to change a little. Not in her behavior or personality, but her body started changing—or, maybe I just started noticing more closely. After college, she developed some distinctive looking curves and her legs somehow were apparently longer and sexier now. It's hard to understand.

We lost track of each other for a few years after college. Mary moved from our old neighborhood into a nice area around Baptist Hospital known as Ardmore--small, well-kept houses, with an eclectic feel about it. I'd see her occasionally when she came back to visit her mom and dad, but we weren't really close like we used to be. I missed her.

Mary works for the Parks and Recreation Department here in Winston-Salem and has the responsibility of maintaining the tennis facility at Hanes Park and several of the other public hard courts around town. As far as I know she's been single and unattached her entire life--except for a dog and a cat. I almost want to say she's normal, but the only normal people you know are the ones you don't know very well. And I know Mary. She's not unattractive, but she doesn't really try to BE attractive either. I don't think I've ever seen her wear makeup or do anything special with her hair. And, except for a couple of funerals and one wedding, I've never seen her in a dress. She's just Mary. Always has been and always will be.

I called several times before she actually answered. She said she was out hiking at Sauratown Mountain—this proves she's not normal. When I told her I would like to come over and talk to her, she said she was busy tonight but tomorrow night would be great. Busy tonight? Doing what? Does she have a date? I tell her I'll see her tomorrow night about 7:00 and we hang up. She doesn't ask me what I want to talk about or seem the least bit curious—which in itself, is curious.

Since Jennifer and her mother are all consumed now with ring shopping, I'm left alone tonight, so I decide to ride around town, just kill some time. Maybe I'll ride by old Mary's house once or twice, or however many times it takes until I can see who she's going out with. The thought of her maybe being a lesbian is sort of exciting to me—in a weird kind of way. After seven trips by her house, she is still at home and no one has come over. Maybe she lied to me. Then, as I'm parked down by the corner, behind a large SUV, I see Mary come out of her house, get in her car, and leave by herself. I'm really excited now—I'm actually going to follow someone, like a private detective would—or policeman—or pervert.

It was actually pretty boring. Mary went four blocks away to the Methodist church, where she parked with about a dozen other cars and then went inside. Hmm, I don't think any lesbian dating is going on here, so I give up and drive through the hamburger place and go back home.

The next day, when I arrive at Mary's house, she has a few healthy snacks set out for us and hands me a bottle of water. Maybe this is why she's still single. Mary is wearing gym shorts, or tennis shorts, I'm not sure which, only that they are short. Mary has better legs than I remember. We catch up on things for a few minutes and talk about some old friends, then I tell her I want to explain some strange occurrences I've had recently. She asks, "Strange occurrences? What does that mean?"

"Exactly what it sounds like...something strange happened to me that I can't explain. And it's happened three different times."

She nods and replies, "I'm sure there's a logical explanation for everything. Maybe it's just something you're not understanding, or not seeing the whole picture."

"Maybe," I say. "I'll tell you exactly what happened, then you tell me if it's normal or not."

So, I begin with the story of the homeless man calling my name outside of Panera Bread and telling me he knows who I am. When I finish, Mary looks at me and says, "Well, obviously, it's someone who used to know you that you've forgotten. Probably someone you worked with years ago, or met somewhere—something like that. I don't see anything unusual about that at all, except your memory is not very good."

I know it's pointless arguing with her; she'll never believe that I truly had no idea who this man was, so I go on to the next story.

When I finish detailing the incident at Panera when the woman walked behind me and spoke to me, Mary once again had a logical explanation. She explained, "Jerry, she probably wasn't even speaking to you. She was probably on her cell phone talking to someone else and you overheard a part of her conversation. You're imagining things that just aren't happening. Neither of these incidents seems strange at all to me."

"Okay. I understand what you're saying, Mary. I don't agree with you, but I understand how you could sense that. I thought about those things as well, but I've never, ever seen that man before, and that woman spoke to ME. She wasn't on a cell phone or speaking with anyone else—only me. And now the weirdest one of all . . ."

After I finished explaining what happened in the jewelry store and the disappearing woman, Mary sat in silence for a moment or two, took a sip of bottled water, then said, "I think you've misremembered something about that story. People just don't appear, then disappear. There's a logical explanation that you've simply overlooked or forgotten."

I look into her eyes and I'm not sure if she really thinks that, or if she thinks I'm a little nuts, or if she thinks I'm just messing with her. We sit in silence for a minute or two and I finally say, "Okay."

Eventually, Mary says, "I didn't say I don't believe you, I just think you didn't entirely see everything about each of these events. There was more going on than was in your field of vision or understanding. And, you know how you are...your imagination can sometimes go off in leftfield somewhere. Trust me, nothing weird is happening to you, Jerry. You're not that special. I mean that in a kind way."

I decided to change the subject. She had her viewpoint, which was wrong, and I knew what actually happened, which was still unexplainable. We talked about Jennifer and I said all the things I was supposed to say. I gave Mary every opportunity in the world to tell me of anyone special in her life, but she chose not to. Instead, we talked about work, her dog and cat, our parents and friends, and all the same kind of stuff friends talk about when there's nothing left to talk about. I finally went home, a bit waterlogged and disappointed in the conversation. I don't know what I expected her to say, but I didn't expect her to say that I was "not that special." But, as I'm quickly learning, it's okay to live a life others don't understand.

Mary called me on my cell phone before I got back home. She wanted to apologize if she'd hurt my feelings or made me mad by not believing my story of strange events. I assured her everything is fine and thanked her for listening. Before she said goodbye, she made this rather odd comment, "I'm glad you stopped by. It was good seeing you and I hope things turn out well with the engagement. It's good spending time with those you love. One of these days you will say either, 'I wish I had' or 'I'm glad I did.' Good night, Jerry."

She hung up before I could understand what she meant; heck, I still don't understand what she meant. Did she mean it was good spending time with her? Or, me spending time with Jennifer? I'm more confused now than before I talked with Mary. But, I am sure of two things: Mary has nice legs, and, now more than ever, I'm certain that what I experienced was real.

5

WEEK AFTER WEEK I dutifully eat my bagel with peanut butter, but occasionally switch between light roasted and dark roasted coffee. Once, I even added a little hazelnut to my blend—I can live on the wild side now and then. I'm fairly disappointed that my life has reverted back to a certain normalcy that I'm almost bored with. But Jennifer seems a little more interested as the fall wedding is getting closer. Or, maybe it's just the idea of a wedding that she's interested in...nah, I'm sure she's interested in me.

Then, just as I've come to grips with my monotonous, repetitive and wearisome lifestyle, a flash of lightening hits. One Thursday morning I park my car and start into Panera for my morning libations when I look up and the homeless black man I'd first met weeks and weeks ago is standing on the curb looking at me, almost as if he's waiting for me. I look directly back at his face and catch his stare in mine, while walking directly up in front of him. When I stop, he says, "Good morning, Jerry. Good to see you again."

"Who are you? And, how do you know me?"

He smiles a little and says, "Jerry, I've always known you. You shouldn't be concerned with trivialities like that. You should be more concerned with your life and what's happening with it."

"What do you mean 'what's happening with it,' and what exactly should I be concerned with? And, how do you know what's happening in my life? And WHO are you?"

He smiled, but said nothing in reply to my questions. He turned to walk away and I asked him, "Where are you going? And what's your name?"

Again, he said nothing at first, but he did stop and turn around to look at me. Then, after a moment or two he said, "Jerry, we're all in the same game; just different levels, dealing with different devils. You know who we are. I'm going to catch the bus now. Pay attention. I'll talk to you later." And with that, he started walking quickly towards the road, where the city bus was just pulling up across the street. I watched him get on the bus and ride away. I walked back to my car, opened the door, got in and started to drive away when I realized I hadn't even had my bagel yet. Dang, what's going on here?

I walk into Panera and stand in line behind a hipster, wearing a Fedora, peg-legged pants and suspenders. He orders some sort of latte, mocha, junk-laden drink and a gluten-free pastry. Over his shoulder, Ida, the assistant manager, catches my glance and rolls her eyes. She's paid to endure even the most ridiculous of requests—it can't be an easy job.

When the Bohemian, New-Age traveler gently saunters away, Ida looks at me and says, "Do you want blueberry or cinnamon/raisin today with your daily dose of peanut butter?"

I look back at her and wink, saying, "Blueberry, and you forgot my coffee, Ida." I'm hoping they have an extra strong blend today that will help me comprehend what just happened outside. Ida is preparing the bagel for me and I ask her if she happened to see me outside just now, talking to an older man.

She replies, "Yes, I did. Who was he? He looks homeless. If he wants to come back later, I can give away a few breakfast pastries that haven't sold. Just tell him to come in and ask for me."

Well, that was nice, but it didn't really answer my question about who this man was. I smile and thank Ida, then take my bagel, peanut butter, and dark roasted coffee back to a corner table so I can think. Or, not.

As I'm buttering the second half of my bagel, and trying to remember my conversation a few minutes ago, it hits me like a sledgehammer. He said, "You know who WE are . . ." You know who "we" are! Was that a slip on his part, or did he really mean "we?" Who is "we?" I suddenly feel like Bill Clinton during his impeachment hearings trying to confuse and explain the different meanings of what "is" is. As with Mr. Clinton, the more I talk and think, the worse it gets. Everything is hard before it gets easy; just eat your bagel, drink your coffee, and remember: silence isn't empty, it's full of answers.

The police called me to say they were dropping the investigation at the jewelry store, but in an unofficial aside they told me it might be a good idea not to shop there for a while. Don't worry about that officer. Jennifer and her mom are as busy as two little bees, planning all sorts of stuff...I hope I don't get stung too hard. From what I'm gathering, they are focusing on a venue up at Blowing Rock for the wedding and festivities. Knowing Blowing Rock as I do, I'm sure it's a fancy, expensive place. But it'll all be worth it when Jennifer walks down that aisle and says "I do." I don't care what Joe says, it WILL all be worth it.

Since Jennifer is so busy now, I have a lot of free time on my hands, so I call up old Mary one night to see if she wants to do something. Not a date—just hang out, like in the old days. She says, "Are you sure it's okay with Jennifer?'

"Of course it is. She knows we're just old friends." And I wanted to add, "and that you're gay," but I didn't. I told Mary I'd pick her up about 6:30 and we'd get something to eat, maybe at our old hangout—The Dairy Ranch.

She said, "Jerry, they closed that place about eight years ago. I know a place we can go. See you at 6:30."

When I pulled up in Mary's driveway she was coming out the front door. She jumped from her porch, over a small bush and four steps to the sidewalk. Same old Mary. She had on baggy blue jeans, an Appalachian State sweatshirt, and pink tennis shoes. Quite a contrast to my khakis, golf shirt, and loafers. Again, Mary had on no makeup that I could tell, but her hair seemed to be spiked down the middle with some sort of jell or spray.

She hopped in and said, "Let's go downtown." So that's where we went. She wanted pizza and suggested Mellow Mushroom, which was fine with me. We split a large: she got goat's cheese, avocados, and mushrooms on her half; I ordered the Meat Lover's—hamburger, pepperoni, steak, sausage, and bacon on my half. Mary ordered a Diet Sprite while I wanted to watch my calories and ordered a Michelob Ultra. We watched the people and cars pass by and tried as hard as we could to be comfortable with each other.

Mary finally said, "I hope you're not mad at me about our talk the other night, but I felt like I had to assure you that none of those instances was anything but a misunderstanding on your part. We all get confused at times and hear things, or think we hear things, that we really didn't."

I didn't want to argue with her, or to ask her to explain the woman in the jewelry store that disappeared, or to explain how the homeless man met me again at Panera. So I searched for a slice of pizza with a large chunk of bacon on it...I always find that when I'm eating bacon, I don't really care what anyone else thinks. Sitting across the table from Mary, in the neon lights of Mellow Mushroom, she had an appearance that made me think,

"With a little mascara and eyeliner, old Mary could probably be attractive, in an athletic sort of way."

But I was jolted back to reality by a text from Jennifer: "Hey honey. What R U doing?" It irritated me a little that with an unlimited plan she still had to abbreviate words.

"Nothing. Having a pizza with Mary."

"Oh."

"How are you and your mom doing?" Two minutes, four minutes, eight minutes...I guess she's not going to answer.

Mary and I finish our pizza. Well, I finish mine. She only ate two of her four slices. She asks if want a piece of hers, and I would if it had something besides avocados, mushrooms, and goat cheese on it. I would've eaten the whole thing! With pizza, I don't stop eating when I'm full. The meal isn't over when I'm full. It's only over when I hate myself. We talked about some old teachers we had in school and about the environment—well, mainly it was her talking about the environment. I was trying to decide if old Mary was wearing a bra or not under that sweatshirt. I don't think she is. There's a little too much bouncing going on as Mary gets excited discussing global warming. Boobs prove that men CAN focus on two things at once.

The environment really got Mary excited; she talked about it all the way home. I tried not to stare too much. As soon as I stopped in her driveway, she hopped out and said, "I had a great time, Jerry. I hope we can see more of each other. Bye." See more of each other? Does she mean see more of each other? Or, see MORE of each other? Hmm.

But my reverie is broken as I receive another text from Jennifer which says, "Call me, now."

I wait until I'm home before calling Jennifer, I feel a little safer here. "Hey, Jenn. What's up?"

"You know I don't like being called Jenn. My parents named me Jennifer."

"Sorry. Is everything okay?"

"So, you had dinner with Mary, right?"

Take a deep breath Jerry, it'll be okay. "Yes, I told you I was meeting a friend for dinner."

"Well, apparently you forgot to mention it was Mary. Don't you think you should've told me you were having dinner with another woman? Or was it a secret?"

"Jennifer, it wasn't another woman, it was just Mary. You know her."

"Yes, I'm afraid I do. All bouncy and jiggly; always running around and being athletic. And I don't think she ever wears a bra either."

"Well, I never noticed that." I lied, "And you know she's gay don't you?"

"Jerry, have you actually ever seen her with another woman? Haven't you ever thought she's just a little too interested in continuing your 'old' friendship? Just because a woman doesn't wear makeup and dresses like a guy doesn't mean she's gay."

I never thought about that. Could Mary NOT be gay? Could she actually be interested in me? We all eat lies when our hearts are hungry. While my mind is whirling with these thoughts, Jennifer continues, "I just don't want you to be misled and get yourself in trouble. Remember, you're almost a married man and it's probably not appropriate for you to be having dinner alone with another woman."

"Okay, no problem. I never thought about it that way. It won't happen again." Silence. More silence. "Are you still there?"

"Yes, Jerry. Call me tomorrow. We've got things to discuss."

"Okay, I will. I love . . ." But before I can finish my profession of love, Jennifer has ended the call. Wow. Things to discuss and Mary might not be gay. That's two pretty intense subjects for me to think about tonight. I hope I'm up to it.

What Jennifer wanted to discuss with me was how much I could contribute for a down payment on the wedding venue. Whatever it takes to make her happy. Then an improbable thought crosses my mind: Can anything make her happy? If we can ever make it through this whole wedding episode, things will be okay. Our lives will get back to normal and we'll all be fine. I'm sure of it.

I'm looking forward to some mental relief as I pull into the Panera parking lot. A hot cinnamon/raisin bagel, peanut butter, and a tasty cup of coffee are exactly what I need to get my mind off all things wedding and braless—no...that's not what I meant. Just wedding. Snap out of it boy.

No line this morning-- it's my lucky day! Not. They are out of cinnamon/raisin and blueberry bagels. All that's left are plain and some sort of sesame seed, cheese flavored millennial bagels. The poor cashier sees the disappointment in my face and apologizes. I don't want a PLAIN bagel! I start to only order coffee, when Ida comes from the kitchen area and sees me.

"Hey, Jerry, good morning."

"Hey, Ida. So, you're out of bagels today?"

"Well, we're not out, but we don't have a big selection left. Wake Forest ordered nearly everything we have for a big meeting they're having."

"Oh. Just give me a cup of coffee then."

"Look, go ahead and get your coffee ready and I'll go in back and get you a blueberry and cook it up real fast. I'll bring it to you before you know it."

"You don't need to do that, Ida. It's okay."

"No problem. Go get your coffee and I'll be right over."

I get my coffee, then walk over to the window just to check if the homeless man may be out there—he's not. I feel a little guilty about Ida cooking me a single bagel, but not that guilty. She brings it to me and sets the tray down while saying something. I wasn't paying attention since my mind was contemplating braless sweatshirts. I finally noticed Ida was still standing there and I looked up at her. When I did, she turned and walked away. Wonder what's wrong with her? I lather up my bagel with peanut butter and think of wedding venues, work, and the environment, then lustily revert back to thoughts of an Appalachian sweatshirt and the revelation it may conceal.

\

6

I HAVE TO GO to Charlotte today for a corporate meeting we do each quarter. These meetings are very boring and the traffic in the city is incredibly horrible. They've been working on the roads in and around Charlotte my entire adult life and they're still terrible. At least twenty-five miles before you get to the city, traffic is stopped on the interstate, which is four and five lanes in each direction. Go a hundred yards and stop, go two hundred yards and stop, repeat this scenario for the next twenty-five miles. Our meeting is actually in Pineville, a suburb of Charlotte, so I decide to exit the constipated interstate and take some back country roads to the meeting site. It may be longer this way, but at least I'll be moving.

The winding back roads alternate between 45 mph and 55 mph. I'm making pretty good time until I see up ahead all traffic is stopped on this two lane road. Looks like some sort of road construction is going on. Four other cars are stopped in front of me and the drivers are all out of their cars standing in a group talking. I stop, get out of my car, and walk up to them. They're discussing the latest NASCAR race and how Dale, Sr. would have won, if he'd only been alive and racing in it.

Eventually, they tell me the state D.O.T. told them it would be about ten more minutes until they opened up the road again. Not being a NASCAR fan, I walk back to my car as I bring up emails and texts from my cell phone. I'm half leaning on the front of the car, reading a text from Jennifer about you know what, when I hear someone yelling in a field off to the side. I look over and a farmer, I guess he's a farmer, is yelling something that I can't understand. He's also pointing frantically to the road behind me. As I turn around to look, I see a car about two seconds away, racing right at us. This car has not slowed down at all. I leap as fast and far as I can towards the ditch off the road just as the speeding car slams into my car.

My car hits the one in front of me causing the next three cars to all hit each other in a chain reaction from the impact. The guys in the group up front weren't hit because the impacts never made it to the front SUV where they were standing. It all happened so fast, it was over before we knew what happened. The guys up front ran back to the car that caused the impact, one of them obviously calling 9-1-1 and the police as he ran. I jumped back across the ditch to the first wrecked car where the air bag was deployed and smoke was venting out. A young girl was behind what was left of the steering wheel and the air bag. She was bleeding all over her face and was either unconscious or dead, I couldn't tell which.

The other guys arrived as I did and they somehow got the passenger side door open and pulled the girl out. Once they had her clear of the car, it was obvious to us she was dead. She had no pulse and there was a gashing hole in the side of her head with her brains oozing out. She looked to be seventeen or eighteen years old maybe. A rescue squad vehicle arrived a few minutes later and as soon as they saw the girl they all shook their heads as well. They covered the girl's body and waited for the police who quickly arrived as well. They listened to our stories of the crash and took our names and phone numbers for insurance purposes.

I told them all I was extremely fortunate to be alive because the farmer warned me of her car coming at us. Only then did I think to look over to where he had stood. I did not see him anywhere in the field and was not in our little group. I looked up and down the road and across the open field but never saw him. The county policeman asked me to describe him so they could interview him, but I didn't remember anything except for some reason I thought he was a farmer. The policeman asked the other guys if they could describe this "farmer" and they each truthfully said they didn't see anyone or hear anyone yelling anything. The policeman said there were no houses anywhere close to where we were and the open field was just a pasture with no cattle, sheep, horses, or farmers in it.

The cop said he'd drive back down the road in each direction and stop to ask if anyone had been there and seen the accident. He wanted an eyewitness to the girl's car before impact. It took all morning before tow trucks came and took our wrecked cars away. I knew my car was beyond repair. I called Jennifer but she was at work and couldn't come to pick me up, so I called my cousin Joe who drove down and took me back home. No meeting for me today.

Joe wanted to know all about the accident and how it happened. I told him everything I could remember, except about the farmer in the field yelling at me and waving. The same farmer that no one else saw or heard. The same farmer who was nowhere to be seen by anyone...but me.

Dealing with the insurance company was frustrating: They would not pay me anywhere near what I thought my car was worth. So, now I have to buy a new car (or used one) and fork out money for a wedding that is getting ominously close now. I hope she doesn't want a big honeymoon.

I receive a text from Mary asking about getting together again for lunch one day. I text back and ask her if she'd like to meet me at Panera Bread tomorrow. I'm not taking her out, I'm not picking her up, I'm just going to Panera for a bagel and if Mary happens to be there, well, it'll just be a coincidence. That's my story. Shut up!

Jennifer is busy with her mom planning this and that, which is fine with me. I don't really care what shade of aqua the invitations are, or if the flower arrangements clash with the wedding dress. Really? When I'm alone, though, I can't stop thinking about that poor, young girl killed in the crash. A life gone, parents devastated, a family mourns and questions "Why?" I did receive an email from the police that said the girl was in the middle of a text to her boyfriend and never even applied the brakes before impact. I also cannot stop thinking about the farmer. I wish someone would send me an email explaining that.

I arrive in the parking lot at Panera before Mary does, so I sit in my loaner car and wait for her...looking for you-know-who. I don't see him. When she pulls in the lot, I get out to meet her at the door and wave as we're both walking up. As we're about ten feet from each other, HE walks out of the door at Panera and holds it open for us to enter. Mary says, "Thank you, sir."

He looks at her, smiles, and says, "Good morning, Miss. Nice to see you on such a beautiful day."

Mary walks in and he looks at me, but only smiles and nods. At least now I know that I'm not the only person who sees him. He's indeed real, but no less mysterious. Mary orders something I've never heard of, but it sounds a little too healthy for me. I stick to my favorites. As we're walking back to a table, Ida waves to me and says, "I saw your friend today and gave him a pastry; he was asking about you."

I wanted to find out from Ida what he was asking so bad I was about to burst—but Mary would never understand. So I'll just burst on the inside. We sat down and Mary said a short prayer while I looked at her sweatshirt. As she arranged everything before her, she looked up and asked, "Who is this friend that was asking about you?"

I could lie to old Mary, or I could say I have no idea, or...I could tell her the truth. I think I'll lie to her. "It was a guy I went to college with. I meet him over here sometimes." She gives me that look that says, "I don't believe you, but I'll let you off the hook this time." We talk about everything except Jennifer and the impending nuptials. Mary is disappointed that I'm not buying a Prius (to help the environment) as a replacement for my wrecked car. I didn't have the courage to tell her I wouldn't buy a Prius even if the North Pole turned into a summer vacation resort.

As I'm coating my bagel with a double layer of peanut butter I notice something different about old Mary. Does she have on makeup? I'm not sure but I think she does, and I'm positive her hair has had something done to it. Uh, oh. Then Mary tells me she has a meeting today with the district supervisor about next year's budget—that's why she's wearing makeup—got to be.

I tell her all about the crash, except for the farmer part, and she is appropriately distressed about the young girl and concerned about how close I came to actually getting hurt. I have a second cup of coffee and Mary has another glass of water as we talk about nothing. It's easy talking about nothing with Mary. We all need a friend who understands what we're not saying. I tell her how I'm concerned about the young dead girl's family and how the wedding is very concerning (that's the best word I could think of). And, I tell her how the general state of affairs in my life and the world worries me a little. Mary nods and looks intently in my eyes saying, "Jerry, I've read the last page of the Bible. It's all going to turn out all right."

I look back at Mary and realize something. I can't identify what that something is—but I know it's something. I could hear a hundred sermons from the greatest preachers in the world, but none would resonate with me as much as those two sentences from my old friend Mary.

We finish our lunch and walk outside to leave, but then I remember I left my cell phone on the chair beside me. We say goodbye and Mary walks to her car...I think her jeans are a little tighter today than usual. I hurry back inside to get my phone and Ida has it in her hand walking towards the door to meet me. "I think you forgot this, Jerry. Your friend must have you really distracted."

"She's not my friend. I mean, not like that; not like a girlfriend. We're just old friends, we grew up together and we're just re-connecting now."

Ida just smiles and nods, replying, "Whatever you say. Have a great day, Jerry."

Well...she IS just a friend. Not a girlfriend. I'm engaged—she is not a girlfriend. And, anyway, she's gay. I think.

As I walk back out the door of Panera, with my cell phone this time, I hold the door open for a frazzled young lady carrying a newborn baby and leading her small daughter by the hand. I smile at them all and look down at this little four or five year old girl and she looks back up at me and says, "You sure you got the right girl?"

Her mother says, "Let's go, Kali," and pulls her inside.

Did I hear her right? Why couldn't Mary be here to witness this? No, I didn't hear that right. She wasn't talking to me. I'm still standing there holding the door open—stunned. I can't take my eyes off the little girl, who is now in line with her mother. As I'm finally ready to close the door, the little girl turns around and looks at me, raising her little eyebrows.

I'm blocking traffic; I have to move out of the way. I let go of the door, but somehow can't compel my feet to move. Ida walks over to me and asks, "Are you okay, Jerry?...Jerry?"

"Yes. Yes, I'm fine. Thank you. See you later, Mary."

"Ida. My name's Ida."

"I'm sorry, Ida. I'm fine, see you later."

7

OKAY, I'M OFFICIALLY spooked now. When a little four year old girl speaks to me, it's time to do something about it. Like what, Jerry? I certainly can't talk to Jennifer about anything except wedding junk. I can't talk to my cousin Joe—I've already tried that. I can't talk to Mary-- she thinks I'm overreacting to these events. I don't want to worry my mother. I have some other friends I go to ballgames with, but not one of those guys is close enough to confide in. I can't go to a psychologist or psychiatrist—I can't afford that with all the wedding and car expenses I've had. I need to talk to a preacher. But you don't go to church Jerry and you don't actually know any preachers. As I'm mulling this over, I'm silently telling my inner voice to shut up.

But Mary goes to church and she knows a preacher. She'll help me. I know good old Mary will help me.

"No, I'm not going to introduce you to my preacher just so you can self-analyze yourself, Jerry." She actually put her hands on her hips as she said that. I'd just dropped by her house unannounced and asked her if I could have a few minutes of her time. She seemed happy to see me and brought me a bottle of water. I just barged right into it and asked her if she could introduce me to her preacher so I could talk to him about some "personal matters." I wasn't prepared for her response-- I thought she would say "yes." And, I wasn't prepared for her to be in shorts with a tank top tee-shirt on—and definitely braless.

She stands there, hands on hips, nipples tight against the thin tee-shirt, waiting for my reply; or maybe waiting for me to make a move on her. Imagination is the true magic carpet ride. She senses my futility and finally says, "Sit down and tell me what's going on."

I do and tell her most of what's going on—I can't tell her everything. I can't tell her of the continued sightings I'm having, or why I'm having to cover myself up below the waist.

I convince her that I need to confide my earlier sightings and incidents to someone who will be discreet, yet understanding. I don't know if she believes this or not, everybody has a little bit of Watergate in them. At this point, I don't know if she's trending Richard Nixon or Sam Ervin. She finally says, "Okay, Jerry, I'll call him for you and see if he has time to see you. Are you telling me the truth about everything?"

"Of course I am, Mary. I can't get these things off my mind. Maybe they are all misunderstandings on my part, but my mind won't rest or let go of them. I need a professional counselor to help me come up with a solution so I can have some peace."

"I'll call him tomorrow and let you know what he says. Do you want me to set up an appointment if he's free?"

"Yes, any time after work is fine with me. Just let me know. Mary, I'm sorry to impose on you like this, I really am."

I get up to leave and Mary steps over to me and hugs me tightly, saying, "It's alright, Jerry. I just wanted to be sure you were serious. You know I'll help you and do anything I can, anytime at all."

Mary hugs really good. Mary smells really good. Mary feels really, really good. I need to get out of this house quickly before the devil inside me starts winning. Inside my car, I notice a text from Jennifer: "Where are you? We need to talk!!"

Two exclamation points? This can't be good. Certainly she doesn't know I'm at Mary's house...does she? I decide to take the safe approach and make up a good story—just in case. I drive over to the gym where I'm a member...but never actually go. I park in the lot and then call Jennifer. She answers on the first ring, not with hello but with, "Where are you?"

"I'm at the gym. What's up?"

"Why are you at the gym? You never go to the gym."

"I just thought I should try to firm up things a little before the wedding. You don't want a fat husband do you?" This sounded like solid, sound reasoning to me.

"Oh, Jerry, you're not fat, you're just easy to see. Now I'm going to talk fast, so listen to me. I need you to call Reverend Mattox and set up a time for us to do marriage counseling---not that we need it, but he requires it to perform the ceremony. I wasn't sure what your schedule is. Then, check out the all-inclusive resorts on Jamaica and book us a week there for our honeymoon. You need to do this now, Jerry, before all the trips are sold out. Then, go get measured for a tux as soon as possible; you don't want to wait until the last minute in case they need to do alterations. Call me tomorrow and let me know how your progress is coming. I have to run."

Silence. "Jerry, did you hear me?"

"Yes, honey, I'll take care of it. I love . . ." She hung up.

Well, at least she let me know where she and her mom decided we'd go on our honeymoon. I wonder if her mom's coming with us? Secondly, I wonder if my credit card has enough left on it to actually make a down payment on an all-inclusive Jamaican resort? Things are starting to move a little too fast for me now. I remember one other thing I've been ordered to do: confirm my best man for the wedding. I call my cousin Joe. He's my closest living male relative, and though he's tough sometimes, I know he loves me like a brother.

"Hey, Joe. How's the best bartender in Winston doing?"

"Are you drunk, Jerry?"

"No, I just wanted to talk to you and see how you're doing."

"Neither one of us believes that. What do you want?"

No use beating around the bush, so I tell him. "I want you to be my best man at the wedding and just wanted to confirm it all with you."

A few seconds of silence, then he asks me, "Do you love this woman with all your heart, Jerry? Would you die for her?"

"Of course I love her, Joe. I wouldn't be marrying her if I didn't love her."

"Jerry, I'm going to ask you a serious question and I'm only going to ask it once...and I want an honest answer. Then, I'll never bring it up again."

"Okay, shoot."

"I want you to think about how this woman talks to you, how she treats you. Does SHE love you more than anything in the world? Would she die for you? Jerry, are you absolutely certain this is the woman you want to spend the rest of your life with?"

I wanted to say "yes" right away. I wanted to assure him Jennifer was right for me. I wanted to convince myself Jennifer was right for me...but I hesitated. I was going to answer "yes"—I meant to answer "yes." But I hesitated.

And with that hesitation, Joe said, "I'm not doing it, Jerry. Life minus love equals nothing! I won't be a part of it. Don't ask me again and for your own sake, and for the sake of that poor girl, walk away now. Goodbye."

Oh, great! What am I going to do now? Jennifer's going to kill me. Not if I don't tell her; no use upsetting her if I don't have to. I'll give Joe a week or two to calm down and I'll ask him again. He'll be fine.

I get a call from Mary telling me the preacher has agreed to see me tonight at 7:00 at his office in the church. She tells me his name is Will Simpson and warns me to be "nice" to him. Really, Mary? You have to warn me to be nice to a preacher?

When I drive up to the church, he's outside picking up some small limbs that have fallen in the yard. I'm not exactly sure how to address a preacher: is it Reverend Simpson, Mr. Simpson, Father Simpson? But before I'm forced to say anything, he calls out, "You must be Jerry, great to see you. I'm Will. C'mon in. Can I get you something to drink?" I decline, but immediately regret my decision when he gets a Diet Mountain Dew from a small refrigerator in his office for himself. Dang.

He's much younger than I imagined. In fact, I think I'm older than he is, which is soon verified when I see a diploma hanging on the wall from Wake Forest University with a recent date. We talk about life in general and mention Mary and my job before he actually gets to the point and asks what it is that I'd like to discuss with him. Rather stupidly, I ask him if everything we talk about is only between him and me. I knew the answer, but I needed confirmation before I told him the WHOLE story. He confirmed and I started from the day I first met the homeless man.

I told him about the woman passing behind me in line at Panera. I told him the entire weird saga of the jewelry store and the disappearing woman. I told him about the farmer in the field at the car accident and I finished by telling him of the little girl at Panera and what she said to me. He didn't interrupt or ask any questions until I finished.

When I did finish, he still didn't say anything for a moment or two, then finally spoke saying, "And..."

"And what?" I answered.

"And, what is the question you want to ask me? The question you're afraid to ask me, but the only question you've come here to find an answer to."

I sat there looking at him, then looking at the floor, then looking at my hands, then finally looking back at him. He never took his eyes off of me. Finally, I got up the courage to ask the question I've been longing to ask, but was afraid to ask, "Were those really angels speaking to me?"

He nodded, took a sip of Diet Mountain Dew, and smiled. Then answered, "I don't know, Jerry, I wasn't there. Do you think they were angels?"

"I have no explanation. I think it was something. Have you ever seen an angel?"

He leaned back in his chair thoughtfully and replied, "No, I don't think I have. But I may have without knowing it. I really don't think an angel would tell you he's an angel if you did meet him. I can tell you this: Scripture assures us angels are all around us to protect us and help us in times of need. So, I do believe they exist."

I ask him further, "Do you believe in angels because of your faith, or have you seen proof of them somehow?"

"Jerry, faith is not belief without proof, but trust without reservation. It's possible you and I, and many others, have personally met an angel. In Hebrews the Bible tells us, 'Do not forget to entertain strangers, for by so doing some have unwittingly entertained angels.' In fact, we read many times in the Bible where angels appeared and were mistaken for men. I truly think angels are actively involved in our lives as Christians on a regular basis."

When he said this he stopped to make sure I was following him, so I ask, "So, you do believe in angels and I could've been contacted by them? Is that right?"

Will smiled a little and continued, "Billy Graham once described angels as 'God's secret agents.' I like that because they're not really out to draw attention to themselves, they're working undercover—that is their role. They are working behind the scenes to protect us, even if we don't know we need protecting. Jerry, we are never alone. Jesus told us he would never leave us or forsake us. That's the most important thing of all. He has promised that His angels are here for us. In dangerous times and in troubled times, the angels of God are with us."

And with that, we both sat in silence for a few moments. I didn't know what else to say or ask. Finally he helps me by asking me a question, "If they were angels, what do you think they were trying to tell you?"

"They weren't TRYING to tell me anything. They told me exactly what they intended to."

"Which was?"

This is the question I was hoping to avoid, but knew I couldn't. "They all made the inference that 'she' was not the girl for me."

Will nodded, then asked, "And you think they were all referring to your fiancée, Jennifer, not being the right girl for you?"

"Yes, I think that's what they all meant."

"Well, Jerry...is she?"

This is the only question I'm not prepared to answer. Not because I don't want to, but because I don't KNOW the answer. So, I silently sit here, wishing I also had a Diet Mountain Dew to sip on. Incredibly enough, at that precise moment, Will gets up, opens the small refrigerator and hands me a Diet Mountain Dew, saying, "Here, you look thirsty."

Will sat back down then asked, "Jerry, are you a believer in Christ?" I was hoping he wouldn't ask me that question. It's not that I don't believe; rather I think it's more that I'm lazy and never think about it. And that I don't think I truly understand what being a Christian means.

So, this is how I formed my response to that question: "I think Christianity has a lot of great points and is a wonderful help to a lot of people, but I have a lot of questions that still need to be answered."

Will nodded, then asked, "What sort of questions?"

I was hoping he wouldn't do that. My mind is trying to come up with something, then it hits me, the same old question all the agnostics and atheists ask: "If Christianity is valid, why is there so much evil in the world?"

Will smiles a little and almost as if he was waiting for that particular question, he answers, "I like to use another example Billy Graham gave once. 'With so much soap around, why are there so many dirty people in the world? Christianity, like soap, must be personally applied if it is to make a difference in our lives.' Jerry, sometimes your only transportation is a leap of faith."

I wasn't exactly sure what that meant, but I nodded approvingly. Then Will asked me an unexpected question: "Tell me about Jennifer, about your relationship, and about how you feel towards each other?"

I started spouting out all the platitudes one is supposed to say about his one and only—Will nodded.

After I finished, Will said, "Jerry, if I was the pastor giving you two pre-marital counseling, this is the question I would eventually ask you? Do you love this person with all your heart and all your soul? And if you're not 100% sure the answer is 'yes,' then maybe you might want to take some time to reconsider your plans."

Before I could say anything, Will continued, "And in response to your question of whether the people you saw were angels or not, I think it's a much more important question to ask yourself if Jennifer is the right woman for me.' You may have seen angels, or you may not have. It may have simply been your subconscious trying to tell you something that you already know. The most important question is not whether you saw angels or not, but do you really think this marriage is the right thing for you both at this point in your lives."

8

MY MEETING WITH THE PREACHER last night didn't really answer any questions I had. In fact, it opened up more questions that I don't think I'm prepared to answer just yet. I was entirely ready to learn something from Will, but I'm not sure I was ready to be taught. At times, the most terrifying thing is to accept oneself completely.

It's a rather cool morning as fall and my upcoming nuptials draw ever closer. After catching up on some invoicing and billing, I take my morning sabbatical to Panera in the hopes a cup of dark roast, hot coffee will give me some inspiration. As soon as I walk in the door, Ida waves at me-- but she's not really waving at me, she's pointing for me to look over towards the corner. He's sitting there.

Without ordering anything, I walk over to the table and look at him. He says, "Have a seat, Jerry. We need to talk."

"Talk about what?"

He smiles at me and gently says, "You know."

I pull out the chair and sit facing him and say, "Before we talk any further, you need to tell me your name, how you know me, and who you are."

Before he can answer, Ida walks up to the table with a cup of coffee and a bagel, saying, "I brought you cinnamon/raisin today, Jerry. I hope that's okay. Can you I bring you anything else, Joel?"

"No, Ida, thanks for everything, I truly appreciate it."

Ida smiles at us and walks away and he continues, "Well, now you know my name, Jerry."

"Okay. Now, who are you? And then, how do you know me?"

"Jerry, it's no mystery or secret. I am who you think I am—a homeless man trying to offer help to the helpless and hope to the hopeless."

"How do you know me? You knew my name...how?"

"Jerry, I hear Ida call out your name every day. You just never noticed me before."

Then, I blurt out something I probably shouldn't have said, but sometimes my tongue goes quicker than my brain: "I thought you were an angel." At first he cracks a little smile, then it evolves into a full blown laugh. And as I watch him laugh, I have the weirdest, strangest thought—how does this homeless man have such perfectly white and straight teeth?

When he calms down I say, "Okay, all that makes sense to me. I just didn't understand things very well."

He looks out the window and says, "Jerry, it's been nice, but I see the bus coming down the street and I have to run—literally." He gets up and gathers his grimy backpack from under the table and takes a step or two towards the door, then turns to me and says, "You really need to pay attention to what Will told you." Before I fully comprehend what he just said, he's out the door and walking briskly towards the bus across the street.

By now my coffee and bagel are cold. Fortunately, peanut butter will still taste good on a cold bagel, but I have to pour out my coffee and get a fresh hot cup. Ida sees me pouring the coffee out and thinks something is wrong with it. She comes over apologizing and I tell her it was fine, but I'd let it get cold while I was talking to Joel. Then I asked her, "How do you know him? Joel?"

"I thought he was YOUR friend. I was being nice to him because of you."

"So you didn't know him before I mentioned him?"

"No, I'd never seen him before. We usually don't let homeless people come into the building unless they are going to buy something. Is everything okay with him? He's not bothering you is he? If he is, I'll call the police."

"No, no, no...he's okay, I just don't understand who he really is."

Ida nods and replies, "Well, he seems to know you and like you; but I guess everybody likes you don't they, Jerry?" She looks up at me and smiles, pats me on the arm, and goes back towards the kitchen.

One of Jennifer's friends has arranged an engagement party for us this weekend. I can't wait. It's at Forsyth Country Club, a place I could never enter unless it's through one of Jennifer's prissy friends. The club itself is very nice, very pricy, and meant to impress—which it does. Jennifer goes over early and I'm to meet her there at 7:00 so we can meet and greet all the people I don't know. Her friend Casey comes with her boyfriend and she looks spectacular. She has on a dress that if one quarter more inch of cleavage showed, you'd say it was slutty. But on Casey, it looked glamorous—I'm sure every other woman there hated her for it.

A small band plays several top 40 golden oldies and soon several people are dancing. Apparently, it's Jennifer's duty to dance with everyone there: the men, so she can flirt with them, and the women so she can gossip with them. I'm standing over near the bar nursing a glass of Chardonnay that tastes like it's been laced with vinegar. I'm not much of a dancer. The band plays a slow ballad and I see Casey and her boyfriend hit the dance floor and start a rather sexually suggestive pas de deux. Seeing Casey dance so provocatively reminds everyone there that everything in the world is about sex, except sex. Sex is about power. And tonight, Casey is the most powerful person in the room.

Before I can get too aroused, Jennifer grabs my arm and says, "Let's dance." I'm trying to remember from my high school prom exactly what I'm supposed to do here. She says, "Hold me tighter." Okay, I can do that. Then she says, "Move your hand closer to my butt." Then I look over her shoulder and see Casey's boyfriend holding her very tight, with his hand nearly on her well-rounded bottom. Now I get it. Jennifer didn't want to dance with me, she just wanted to out-dance Casey. It didn't work.

I switch from sour tasting Chardonnay to a Bud Light, but before I drink much of it Casey invites me to dance with her when the next slow song comes around. I don't mind at all. We make some small talk while we dance and I keep my hands conspicuously away from her butt, because I know, somewhere in this room, Jennifer is looking at me. I tell Casey that it really looks as though she and her boyfriend are truly in love. She replies, "He's not the kind of guy to expose his emotions very easily. I think he loves me, but he's never actually said it yet. However, although love may be the answer, while we're waiting for the answer, sex raises some pretty good questions." From that point, till the end of the song, I don't remember much.

Jennifer didn't request any more dances from me; there are other more important people for her to mingle with. I was enjoying sipping my Bud and watching the others make fools of themselves. A lot of men THINK they can dance...they can't. Whereas most women look sexy and provocative when they move; men, as a whole, look like our underwear is riding up on us and we're trying to straighten it out.

50

As I'm trying to think of a good way to exit early, a younger, plain-looking girl comes up to me and asks if I'll dance with her. I figure she's someone's sister or daughter maybe, so not wanting to hurt any feelings, I acquiesce. Fortunately, an old Beatles' tune is playing and I know it's not very long. I can make it through this. She never says a word or tells me her name. At the end of the song, she starts to pull away, then looks up at my face and says, "Leave her now, before it's too late." She squeezes my hand a little, then turns and walks back towards a group of woman gossiping about something—or someone.

Casey's boyfriend is at the bar getting them drinks, which leaves Casey temporarily alone. I move towards her and say, "Hey Casey, can you tell me who that younger, plain looking girl is over there with those women?" I point in the general direction of the gossiping women, but I don't see the girl I just danced with.

Casey said, "Which one? None of them is very young."

I look to the left, then to the right, then back at the group of women---she's nowhere to be seen.

"Oh, it's okay, I think I know who she is. Thanks anyway."

Where did that girl go? What did she mean? I touched her, I held her hand, I danced with her, and I smelled her perfume, so I know this girl wasn't an angel. She was a real person, not a spirit. But where is she?

Jennifer told me she was going to stay and help clean up. Doesn't the country club staff clean things up? Oh well, I wanted to go home anyway. I went to say goodbye to her. She was standing with a group of women and said, "Here he comes, my Prince Charming. How are you darling?"

How do I answer that? "Great, what a nice party. Are you sure you don't need me to stay and help? I'll be glad to." Please say "no."

"No, we'll be fine. You go home and get your rest. I know you've had a busy week at work. I'll see you tomorrow."

Then she walks over to me, puts her arms around my neck and kisses me deeper and longer than I ever remember. If we could somehow arrange an audience for our bedroom, I bet things would really be spicy.

9

ANOTHER DULL WEEK at work, another week closer to THE DAY. Another week at Panera and not seeing Joel or anyone weird. I got a text from Mary asking if I want to go hiking with her Saturday. Hiking? I wonder if she'll be wearing her Appalachian State sweatshirt. Hmm. I know Jennifer's friends are giving her a bridal shower Saturday, so I'm free and clear—and Jennifer will never know what I'm doing. Hiking and sweatshirts sounds great to me!

I drive over to Mary's house and she tells me to park out front, she'll drive today.

"Where are we going?" I ask. "Stone Mountain, Pilot Mountain, Sauratown?"

Mary says, "No, we're going up to Deep Gap and hike a new trail that will eventually end up at the New River Gorge. You'll love it. Did you bring your hiking boots with you?"

I was wearing my hiking tennis shoes. She sensed that immediately and continued, "You'll be fine. Let's go."

It was an unusually warm Indian summer day, the kind that is becoming less and less frequent as autumn arrives. I noticed old Mary had a cooler and basket of food in the back seat-- she's a good, old girl. Deep Gap wasn't that far away, maybe an hour and a half from Winston up Hwy 421. We passed the sign honoring Doc Watson and found the trailhead parking lot deserted, except for us and a deer and fawn nibbling at some bushes. They soon left us alone to trudge into the wilderness.

The trail followed a meandering stream as it wound through the woods between several rounded peaks. I had no idea where it went, or how long it would take us to get there. I let Mary lead the way, first, because she knew what she was doing; and, second, I liked the view behind her. She carried a small backpack with some water in it and a few snacks. We would stop occasionally and drink some water and she would describe all the various trees and bushes to me. I pretended to understand and actually care about all the trees and bushes. Mary had on a long-sleeved tee shirt and was obviously wearing a bra today; but, she did have on rather skimpy hiking shorts, so not all was lost.

I'm not sure how long we walked, I'm sorry—hiked; but I was getting a little tired. Then we rounded a curve in the trail and right in front of us was a pool of water, with the little stream we'd been following cascading into it. It was quite sudden and quite beautiful. Mary knew about it, but didn't tell me; she wanted it to be a surprise. It was. She said, "Let's take a dip in the water. It's not too cold yet."

Before I could respond, she took off her long-sleeved tee shirt to expose the bathing suit she was wearing underneath. So, it's a bathing suit top and not a bra. Isn't that interesting? Then she slips off her hiking shorts and boots to reveal the rather scanty and slight bottom to her bikini bathing suit. She wades into the water, which is cold, as a mountain stream should be, and says to me, "C'mon in, it's great." I knew it wasn't great, it was cold, plus I did not have a bathing suit on underneath like she did.

She said, "Ahh, c'mon in Jerry. Take your shorts off, I won't look. I'll turn around."

Well, maybe she would turn around, and maybe she wouldn't. The bigger issue for me was the effect cold water would have on my manhood. Nope. I'll stay right where I am.

"I've been fighting off a cold all week, I'd better not get a chill." I lied.

She knew it was a lie, but let it pass. She dipped completely in the frigid water, and floated on her back some. I soon discovered that cold water has the opposite effect on a woman's nipples than it does to a man's privates. Quite the opposite effect! She frolicked a bit longer, then decided she'd had enough. She could've stayed in the water a little longer as far as I was concerned. She got out and dried off with the small towel she'd brought, then said, "I'll be right back."

She went back into the bushes and took off the wet bikini and put back on her shorts and long-sleeved tee shirt. I was looking forward to the hike back.

But old Mary had another surprise for me before we started back. She gathered up a few small twigs and sticks and started a small fire by the pond. She said, "Let's warm our hands before we start back." We sat there while Mary warmed her hands, which had to be freezing from being in that water. I drank some bottled water and ate some raisins and nuts Mary brought along. After a few minutes, Mary said, "Jerry, I just love that we've reconnected. It's special to me that we still get along and that you want to spend time with me. One friend can change your whole life."

"I love it, too. We know each other so well, there's no awkwardness and it's easy to talk to you...I like it."

We both sat there sipping water and enjoying the comfort that old friendship can bring. No words spoken, none needing to be spoken. I really, really like old Mary. And, she truly knows how to wear a long-sleeved tee shirt. As we sit silently and stare into the fire, I'm wondering to myself in just what capacity and definition it is that I'm beginning to like old Mary. We eventually snuff the fire out and water it down, then start back for the car and home.

When we arrive at Mary's house, and my car, she pulls in her drive but doesn't turn the motor off. She doesn't say anything; we both just sit there looking straight ahead at the side of her house—which needs painting, by the way. Finally, old Mary reaches over and takes my hand and says, "Thanks for coming today, Jerry. It means a lot to me."

Before I can answer, she opens her car door and starts unloading the cooler. When I get out, Mary's cell phone rings and she looks at me and says, "I'd better take this. Let's get together again soon, okay?"

I smile and nod as she starts speaking in her phone. You bet we will, Mary. You can count on it.

Jennifer and I go out to dinner at Spring Garden restaurant, downtown, because she knows I'm paying, but the only conversation at our table is between Jennifer and her mother on the phone. Details and more petty details of the wedding: the cake, the invitations, the reception, the band, the gowns, the bridesmaids...on and on and on. At least they had a good wine from Denis Vineyards I'd never tried before. It was good and sweet and full-bodied...it made me think of Mary. Four more weeks, then I promise—no more thinking of Mary. I'll be happily married in four more weeks. Married to the girl of my dreams in four more weeks. Four more weeks. Really, little voice in my head? Only four more weeks?

I couldn't get away from the office until 11:00 Monday morning, and by that time I was developing a caffeine deprived headache and desperately needed a peanut butter fix. After I parked at Panera, I looked all around to see if anyone was waiting on me. Please, no visitors today, just let me fulfill my caffeine fix and satisfy my PB addiction. No one outside and no one inside waiting to talk to me. I'll definitely get the dark roast blend today—two cups.

I drink about a quarter of the cup of coffee before tasting my butter slathered bagel. Is it possible to actually be addicted to these things? I'm trying to convince myself that it's not really possible when I hear a woman's voice. It's Ida: "Hey Jerry, I thought you'd forgotten about me today."

"I'd never forget you, Ida." She smiles hearing that. Then I add, "I couldn't make it through the day without some dark roast coffee and a bagel—you know that." Her smile quickly fades. That didn't come out exactly as I'd planned.

Ida forces another half-smile and before she walks away she says, "I'm glad the coffee makes you happy, Jerry. I hope you have a nice day."

After work, I stop by the bar where my cousin Joe works. He sees me walk in, looks at me and says, "No."

"What do you mean 'No.' I haven't even asked you anything. Maybe I just wanted to have a drink with my best bud."

"No, Jerry. You came here to ask me again about being your Best Man, and the answer is still NO."

"C'mon, Joe, don't be that way. Jennifer would really be disappointed if you back out. I would, too."

He looks at me disgustedly and says, "I doubt Jennifer even remembers who I am. And as far as you're concerned, I'm doing you a favor. If you can't find a Best Man, maybe you'll call the whole thing off—which you should, you lazy, worthless bum."

"No need to call me names, Joe."

"I should call you a whole lot worse than that. You're gonna screw up your sorry, insignificant, meaningless life—which you deserve, by the way—and, you're gonna screw up this girl's life as well. She probably thinks you love her more than anything in the world—which you don't. Do you, Jerry? If your dad was still around he'd kick some sense in your lazy butt—which is what I should do."

"Joe . . ."

"I don't want to hear it, Jerry. You need to get out of here before I hurt you. I don't want to, but I will if you keep up this marriage nonsense."

He walks to other end of the bar and I shuffle out the door, ignoring the two drunks who've become stupefied by our conversation. I honestly had no intention of bringing up the Best Man thing tonight. I only wanted a cold drink and a place to reflect on thoughts of sweatshirts and bikinis.

Completely disheartened, I walk outside the bar and a well-dressed man, who is holding a large bag of something in one of his arms, stops me and asks if I have change for a dollar for the parking meter. I'm pretty sure I don't, but I do have two quarters in my pocket which I give to him, saying, "Here you go, my pleasure." I hand him the two quarters and he takes them in his free hand, then looks at me and says, "Thanks." A second later, he extends his hand to shake my hand, the same hand he was holding the two quarters in—that aren't there anymore. Before I can respond to this incongruity, he says, "Don't make a big mistake, Jerry." And he walks in the bar.

No, no, no, no, no...almost immediately I follow him inside the bar but don't see him. The two drunks I'd just passed were still sitting there and I asked them, "A man holding a large bag just came in here. Where'd he go?"

They looked at me as if I was speaking Chinese to them. I looked around and saw an overweight, professionally dressed woman at the bar drinking a glass of wine. I took three steps over to her and asked her the same question.

"Holding a large bag?" She said.

"Yes, he just walked in about fifteen seconds ago carrying a large bag. Where did he go?"

She looked at me said, "What was in the bag?"

"I don't know—what difference does it make what was in the bag? Did you see him or not?"

"No, I didn't see him." She sneered, "Why would anyone come into a bar carrying a large bag? Are you sure you haven't been drinking with those two?" She said this as she was pointing over towards the two drunks.

Disgustedly, I said, "Thanks for nothing!" I walked towards the restrooms and I looked in the men's room—empty.

I walked back in the bar area and Joe looked at me said, "What are you doing, Jerry?"

"Did you see that man carrying...forget it; nothing. See you later." Where did he go? Where did those two quarters go? This type of thing is happening way too often now. Either I'm losing my sanity, or something or somebody is trying to tell me something. I walked back toward the woman at the bar who was drinking wine and stopped to apologize to her for being a jerk.

She set her wine glass down, turned to me and said, "Do you know why your dog is happier than you?" This made so little sense to me that I didn't know how to respond, so I just turned and walked away. Disappearing quarters, a vanishing man, and an insane question. What can happen next?

10

LESS THAN THREE WEEKS of freedom left. Why am I thinking like that? I love Jennifer, she loves me...I think. But these unexplained encounters are becoming extremely disquieting and much too frequent. I know something is happening that I can't explain and I think it's supernatural. I've got to get more information from Will, the preacher. I don't think he really believed me when we last spoke, but these chance encounters are not accidental and I'm not misinterpreting anything.

I'll call Mary tonight and tell her I'm going to contact Will again, just as a courtesy to her, and because I like hearing her voice. Incredibly enough, I made it in and out of Panera without any paranormal occurrences today. Just a normal coffee and bagel day, except that when Ida saw me, she didn't wave or speak...she was probably busy. The day was boringly long and uneventful. Jennifer asked if I wanted to drop by and help her do something—I wasn't paying attention—but used "a little sick" as a good excuse to not go over. I think she was happy.

I called Mary on the drive home after work—no answer. Then, I swung by her house and her car wasn't in the driveway. Hmm. I went home, ate something, checked emails, and called Mary again—still no answer. This is odd. Is old Mary out on a date? I'll call her later; now I've got to call the preacher, Will, and see if he has any time to see me again—to see if he'll even agree to see me again. Incredibly, he answered immediately and asked if I could come over to his house now. I wasn't expecting that. He gave me directions and I drove right over.

Will and his family of two small kids and a frazzled-looking wife live in a nice little development near Wake Forest. Tree-lined streets, sidewalks and just far enough away from campus so that the fraternity/sorority partying doesn't disturb them. Will greets me at the door holding some sort of spaceman toy in one hand. He sets it down, and leads me into his small office, and shuts the door. He seems rather serious, or maybe he's just not too happy about someone taking up his "family time," especially someone who's not even a member of his church. I don't blame him and suddenly I'm feeling a bit guilty.

He dispenses with any pretenses of daily banalities and gets directly to the point asking, "What can I do for you, Jerry?"

Taking his lead, and not wanting to waste any more of his time, I get directly to the main issue. I tell him of all the repeating occurrences and the bizarre natures surrounding them: strangers knowing my name, quarters disappearing, people disappearing. He doesn't interrupt, or smile, or do anything except keep his stare directly in my eyes.

When I finish, I pause and then say, "Will, something's happening here. I can't explain it. And, I'm not imagining it."

Instead of trying to somehow explain these events, he nods thoughtfully and says, "I want to meet this Joel. He seems to be the instigator or, at the least, he's the only figure who has a recurring role."

"I have no idea how to contact him; I think he's homeless—unless he's an angel, then you'd know better than me how to contact him."

Will replies, "I'm not saying he's an angel, I'm just saying I want to meet him. I have no idea what an angel looks like or sounds like, but I agree with you that something odd or different is happening, and I do think this Joel person knows something that could help us."

I like that Will just used the pronoun 'us' instead of 'you.' I say, "I never know when I'm going to see him, he just appears at times when I'm not expecting him. I'm not sure, but I sort of doubt he'd agree to meet you."

Will thinks a moment then says, "Okay...do this. Keep my cell number handy in your contacts list, and the next time you see him, text me immediately and I'll stop whatever I'm doing—unless it's a funeral...that's a joke, Jerry. I'll come over to wherever you are as quickly as I can. I've got to meet Joel and get a sense of his presence for myself. Plus, if he is an angel, well...wow!"

This sounds like a good plan to me; I'd love for Will to meet Joel. Maybe Joel and he will have some sort of angelic bond together.

As I'm thinking about this, Will asks me, "Have you given any more thought about your faith, Jerry? Maybe inviting Jesus into your life would settle some of the issues you're experiencing."

I'm not sure how to answer this. I truly have not given any more thought about Jesus or my faith—if I even have faith in anything. However, I don't want to hurt Will's feelings, or alienate him, so I say, "Yes, I've thought quite often about it, Will; it's something I'd like to explore and learn more about." Upon hearing this, Will's face brightened and he sat up straight in his chair—I should've kept my mouth shut. Instead, I continued, "I really don't understand Christianity very well and whenever I talk to people about it, they always seem to debunk Jesus and it's hard to know what's real or not real."

Will nodded and picked up a pen off his desk and tapped it several times before answering. Then he replied, "Jerry, the problem with the world, as I see it, is that the intelligent people are full of doubt, while the stupid ones are full of confidence. I heard a very simple explanation once that makes sense to a lot of people: You're born. You suffer. You die. Fortunately, there's a loophole." Having no idea what Will was referring to at this moment, I just nodded and kept silent. He continued, "Our society strives to avoid any possibility of offending anyone— except God. Christians are persecuted for living their faith and ridiculed for believing the Bible. It's apparently okay to do anything and believe anything—except the Bible. It's hard times we live in, Jerry."

I want to just keep nodding and remain silent, but I feel Will wants me say something. Again, all I can think of is the common excuse most people use, "Well, why do bad things happen to good, Christian people? I don't understand that, Will."

He was apparently waiting for this one. He explained, "Jerry, think of your life, in its entirety, as a huge battleship. Each piece of steel used to make that ship—by itself—would sink. But put them all together and when the last rivet is in place—the ship floats! Our lives are like that. One tragedy, or illness, or death, or anything else taken by itself could sink us. But take EVERYTHING as God's purpose for our lives as a sum total— and we will float. You must have that faith, Jerry. To know that in the end, everything will be okay."

Will continued talking, but at this moment, my mind went back to what Mary told me, "Jerry, I've read the last page in the Bible. Everything will be alright."

I'm shaken back to the present when Will walks around his desk next to me and says, "Thanks for coming over Jerry, and remember, text me the very next time you see Joel so I can come and meet him. Okay?"

Two days, three days—nothing. Then on the fourth day since my meeting with Will, I drive into the lot at Panera and I see Joel, the homeless man-- AKA: angel, spirit, ghost, apparition, or whatever he is-- standing near the doorway to the bakery. I'm so nervous, or excited, I drop my cell phone between the seat and the console and I can't reach it. I was hoping to text Will and tell him Joel is here, BEFORE I got out of the car. But as hard as I strain and stretch, I can't reach my phone without getting out of the car, then reaching under the seat. Joel probably saw me drive up; he'll definitely see me get out of the car and use my phone—Dang!

I try to slip out of the car unobtrusively, but when I look over, Joel is looking directly at me. I'm not going to blow this opportunity. I find Will's number then type, "Panera-come quick." If I could text as fast as a teenaged girl Joel might not have noticed what I was doing, but my thumbs simply can't do that. After hitting send, I walk up to Panera and stop in front of Joel, saying, "Good morning. How about a cup of coffee and something to eat?"

"No," he says, "I'm fine." We both nod and look at each other, then he continues, "When will he be here?"

Oh crap! "Who?" I ask.

"Whoever it was that you just texted to tell them I was here."

Should I lie to an angel? "I didn't text anyone about you. I was telling my girlfriend that I love her."

"Jerry, we both know that's not true—neither part of it. How long until he gets here? I don't have all day."

"You'll stay and meet my friend?"

"Of course I will; I have nothing to hide."

I look over at him and boldly ask, "You are an angel, aren't you, Joel?"

"Is that what you think, Jerry?"

"Yes, it's exactly what I think. Just answer the question and tell me the truth. Are you an angel?"

Joel tilts his head a bit and replies, "I'll answer that question if you can answer 'YES' to any of my five questions to you:

Have you ever seen an angel drink coffee, like you and I did?

Have you ever seen an angel eat a pastry, like I did with you?

Do you think an actual angel would ever have need to ride a bus?

If I was an angel, do you think I'd be dressed like this?

And finally, Jerry, do you really, honestly think marrying Jennifer is the right thing for you to do?"

We both stared at each other for a few minutes as I thought about the consequences and repercussions of my answers. Fortunately, I see Will drive into the parking lot, and Joel says, "There he is."

Will quickly gets out of his car and walks over to us. I say, "Will, I'd like you to meet my friend Joel. Joel, this is Will, my preacher friend."

Will says, "I'm honored to meet you, Joel. I've heard a lot about you."

Joel smiles, a bit goofily, and replies, "Same here Mister Will. Mister Jerry says if I dance for you, you might have a couple of dollars for me." And with that he starts doing some sort of Chubby Checker type twist, with a bit if Irish folk dance mixed in. He's humming to himself, dancing up a storm and smiling as broad as he can at Will. Then he starts chanting, "This here dance is for Will, Mr. Will, Mr. Will. This here dance is for Will, Mr. Will, Mr. Will."

Will gathers himself and says, "That's enough, Joel. I appreciate it, but no need to keep dancing. Is there anything else you'd like to tell me?"

Joel immediately stops dancing and smiling, then looks down at his feet and says, "I guess you caught me, Mr. Will, being a man of God and all. I admit that I stole that banana from the market, but I'll make it up to them. I'll sweep the floor and clean the windows to make up for my sin. I swear it, Mr. Will. Please don't hold it against me...I was just so hungry." Joel then hugs Will and starts crying on his shoulder, repeating, "Please forgive me, Mr. Will, please forgive me."

When Joel stops crying, Will pulls his wallet out and hands him ten dollars, saying, "Here, Joel, get something to eat. And please, come by our church and visit the food pantry we have there...here's my card with the address."

Joel starts crying again, thanking Will for his generosity while backing down the sidewalk. We both wave as he rounds the corner of the shopping center and disappears from our view. I'm thinking, "Give me a break!"

Will looks at me and says, "Angel? Really, Jerry? You think HE is an angel?"

I tried to get Will to come inside and have a cup of coffee, but he was either too disgusted with me, or too busy at church, so he declined. I go in by myself and as soon as I place my order I see Ida at the other end. I wave to her, but she sort of half smiles and walks back into the kitchen area. As soon as I sit down, my phone beeps with a text—maybe it's from Will. Wrong-- it's from Jennifer. We're having dinner with her mother tonight at Fratelli's...perfect, I'll try to increase my credit limit before we get there.

My so-called angel friend turns out to be a hobo and a dancing fool, my preacher friend thinks I'm a fool, Ida thinks I'm a jerk, and my fiancée thinks I'm made of money. And, she thinks I love her and her bossy mother. Did I just have a revelation?

As I try to convince myself that I really do know what's happening, I'm quite certain that I don't. I seem to have had more trouble with myself lately than with any other man I know of. The peanut butter soothes me, the coffee revitalizes me. I know what I have to do. I delay a little longer, hoping Ida comes out of the kitchen, but I can't wait. Life goes faster than you think. I walk out to my car, unlock it, and suddenly I feel a tap on my shoulder. I turn around and Joel is standing there smiling at me.

"Well, that was quite an act you put on back there. I didn't know you could dance so well."

"Oh, I can do lots of things, Jerry. Before I go, I want to congratulate you on doing the right thing."

"What right thing?" I ask.

"You know. Jerry, love life and it'll love you right back."

Joel turned to walk away and I called out to him, "You never answered my question."

"Yes, I did. And, Jerry, be in love with your life, every minute of it."

Joel walked away, I went back to work, and Jennifer and her mom are primping for an expensive Italian meal tonight that is not going to happen.

11

I WAS SUPPOSED TO BE at Jennifer's house at 6:30 to pick her and her mom up for dinner. I can't marry Jennifer. I knew I couldn't; all my friends knew I couldn't. I tried to convince myself that I could, but the harder I tried, the worse it got. I had to finally admit to myself that I couldn't remember Jennifer ever saying she loved me. That should be enough—right? Additionally, I truly don't think we actually "like" each other. And why am I always thinking about Mary now? That can't be good.

I hate to ruin their evening, but I'll never make it through tonight knowing what I know. I drive over to her house and knock on the door. Jennifer opens it and says, "You're not going with us dressed like that!"

"Jennifer, I'm not going at all. We need to talk."

She must have known because she burst out crying and wailing. Her mother came to see what was happening, and when she understood, she started cursing me. Then Jennifer started cursing me and said, "I'm keeping the ring," as she ran into her bedroom. Her mother, in between curse words, told me they'd send me a bill for all the expenses they'd incurred and that I WOULD pay it or they'd sue me. Neither one of them ever asked me why or demanded an explanation. I felt bad for Jennifer, she really is a nice person. No, I can't lie about her—she's really not a nice person.

On the way home I felt relieved, unburdened, unincarcerated, and free of guilt—I felt like I wanted to call old Mary. When she answered, I told her what just happened—well, most of it anyway. She asked if I wanted to come over and talk about it. I really didn't want to talk about Jennifer, but I did want to talk to Mary, so I said yes. Mary thought I was distraught and angry and hurt and emotionally spent over the whole episode. I was not. But it felt good knowing Mary wanted to comfort me.

She made us hot tea. I'm not kidding...hot tea! She sat next to me and put her arm around my shoulder from time to time to comfort me. Mary had on an old pair of sweat pants and a loose fitting fleece top with University of Santa Cruz printed on it. I wasn't wondering why a woman in North Carolina was wearing a University of Santa Cruz sweatshirt; I was wondering if she was wearing anything underneath that sweatshirt. I know I should not be thinking those thoughts just after breaking off my engagement, but it's amazing how a little tomorrow can make up for a whole lot of yesterday.

We talked and drank tea. It wasn't as bad as I thought it would be. In fact, if you put in enough sugar, it's okay. Mary said, "It'll probably take you a while to get over this and mend your broken heart; just know that I'm always here for you. Anytime you need to talk, or anything, just call me."

I wonder what ". . . or anything" means? And I know I definitely don't need to tell her that my heart is not broken; in fact, it's leaping for joy and lusting for what's underneath a University of Santa Cruz sweatshirt. I found that if I sound a little broken up, Mary will put her arm around me. And, if I make my voice quiver a little bit, old Mary will give me a hug. It's fun hugging Mary. She kept wanting to know details of why Jennifer and I broke up, and I didn't feel as though I could tell her the truth. Finally, to assuage her inquisitiveness, I simply told her that Jennifer and I were just a little too weird for each other. Different goals, different lifestyles, different aspirations...just not a lot in common.

I got another hug from this comment, then Mary said, "I understand. We're all a little weird. And life is a little weird. But when we find someone whose weirdness is compatible with our weirdness, we join up with them and fall into mutually satisfying weirdness. That is what we call love, Jerry—true love.

Each day when I wake, life truly seems better now. The coffee tastes richer and smoother, and the peanut butter exudes a flavor the Jif people never imagined. My bartender cousin, Joe, is even nice to me. He sent me a text asking me drop by soon. Even Ida is starting to talk to me again. I'm not sure what I did to her, but she'll be fine. Yesterday, as I was buttering up the second half of my bagel, she walked up to my table and asked, "Where's your homeless friend been lately? Did he move on somewhere else for the winter?"

"I'm not sure, Ida, I think he was probably just passing through here. I appreciate you being so kind to him."

Ida smiled at me and replied, "My mama always told me, 'Ida, work hard and be nice to people.' And I've always tried to. See you tomorrow, Jerry."

I was looking forward to Thanksgiving and having some time off. It seemed as though a cloud had been lifted and everything was sunny now. The only negative is that I keep getting phone calls from "unknown sender," and every time I answer, they hang up without speaking. It started with just one or two a day, now I must get four or five of these calls every day and night. I guess I'm going to have to change my number. At first, I thought it might have been Jennifer, but I'm pretty sure if it was her-- she would've started cursing me instead of hanging up.

The only other disappointment is that Mary keeps treating me like I'm heartbroken over Jennifer. She keeps wanting me to discuss my "feelings" and vent my frustrations. I'm ready for her to stop treating me like a "friend-in-need" and more like a "friend-in-lust." Hopefully, time will take care of that.

Mary invites me over to her house once or twice a week and she usually prepares something simple, like grilled cheese or tacos, and we watch television or listen to music. She likes country music and I have to pretend that I do as well. She told me to come over one day after work and I arrived earlier than she expected. I rang the doorbell and knocked several times. After several minutes she opened the door while standing behind it trying to hide herself as much as possible. She'd been in the shower and her hair was wrapped in a towel and she had another towel half-wrapped around her body.

When she closed the door, she started back to her bedroom and told me to give her a few minutes to get ready. Just before she turned from the hallway into her bedroom, either the body towel slipped off or Mary pulled it off early—I'm not sure. What I am sure of is that old Mary has a nice looking bottom. I didn't mention anything, and neither did she, but I kept wondering all night if she "accidentally on purpose" meant for me to see her derriere. It was fun thinking about that.

When Mary was dressed and came out, she asked me how I was coping. She wanted me to tell her about my feelings. She assured me everything would be okay. Take your time, I told myself. Just be yourself...only, cooler. I told Mary what she wanted to hear, biding my time, inching closer to the day when I could see what was underneath those sweatshirts.

Since I ended things with Jennifer, I've not seen Joel or had any other unexplained events with strangers. My life was back to the same old routine, except for the time I was spending with Mary, which was still in the "friendly" stage. Then, one day at work, the manager of our company called me into his office to discuss something with me. His name is Art, and he's been with the company a long time. We get along well and Art trusts me and is not threatened by me at all—he knows I am not the ambitious, pushy type who might be after his job. He knows I take care of everything and keep all our customers happy.

Art told me our company had just won the waste disposal contract at the University of South Carolina in Columbia, S.C., which was the same sort of deal we have with Wake Forest here in Winston-Salem. Wake was my biggest account and I made sure their operation ran smoothly. Art knew this, and he also knew that everything was set up so well that the account could probably do without my day-to-day attention any longer. He wanted me to move to Columbia and set up the type of operation at the university there that I had done with Wake Forest. It would be a nice pay jump and more responsibility, and I'd still be reporting to him.

Art knew I'd recently broken off my engagement with Jennifer and thought now would be a good time for me to "start over" as he put it. They were going to hire a new person, but after the engagement was off Art thought I might like a change. He made it clear that I didn't have to take the job, but there probably wouldn't be this type of opportunity again any time soon. It was a very nice pay raise. He told me to take a week to think about it, then let him know. It is a big decision for me. I've always lived in Winston. It's my home: my mother is here; Joe is here; I like my house, my friends and my life. And, Mary is here.

I left Art's office and went straight to Panera to think about the offer over some light roast coffee and a cinnamon/raisin bagel. Nobody in line today-- that's pretty strange. I place my order with the cashier and I see Ida coming out from the kitchen area smiling at me. "Hey Jerry, good to see you. Your friend is over in the corner waiting on you."

No. No, no, no, no no! As I'm hesitating to look over, because I know who's there, Ida says again, "Over there, Jerry. He's waiting on you."

I pick up my order, fill my coffee cup with dark roast instead of light roast—I'm going to need it-- then look over to the corner with the faint hope the "friend" I'm hoping isn't there is truly not there. Dang! Joel is smiling and waving for me to come over.

I set my tray down, look at him, and say, "Why are you here? And, what do you want?"

"Well, good morning to you as well, my friend. It's good to see you again."

Before I butter my bagel (with peanut butter) I tell him, "I didn't think I'd ever see you again. I thought you'd probably gone back to Katmandu, or Timbuktu, or Kalamazoo, or, in your case, heaven."

He smiled at this comment but didn't say anything in reply. He just kept smiling at me. I decided to wait him out. I buttered my bagel, sipped my coffee, and stared at him as he kept smiling at me. I had all day—sort of. But, I was not going to let him win. I ate the first half, then slowly buttered the second half of my bagel. I took one bite, then went to get a refill of my half empty coffee cup. When I sat back down, the smile had gone from his face and his stare was a bit more intense...if that's possible. He still never spoke as I finished my bagel and drank all the coffee I could comfortably handle.

After a suitable time of reflection for each of us, he nodded and pushed his chair back to rise from the table. He reached down and picked up his grimy backpack, pushed the chair back to its position, and took two steps over to my side and stopped. I did not look up at him. He then said, "You're not moving anywhere, Jerry."

I looked up. He smiled again and walked away, out the door, towards the bus stop across the street.

"Jerry? Jerry? Are you okay?"

"Yeah, Ida. I'm fine."

"Well, you haven't moved for about fifteen minutes. Are you sure you're okay?"

"Fifteen minutes? What do you mean? I was just talking to Joel."

Ida looked very curiously at me and replied, "I know, he left fifteen minutes ago."

12

"MARY, CAN I COME OVER? I really need to talk to someone, someone I can trust."

"Sure, Jerry, give me about thirty minutes and then come on over. What's this about? It sounds serious. It's not Jennifer is it?"

"No, not Jennifer. It's something else. I'll see you in about thirty minutes."

I was at her house in twenty minutes. Mary handed me a bottle of water when I came in and asked if I was hungry. Well, not that kind of hungry.

We sat together on the couch and she said, "Okay, what's this about?"

No more time for me to be coy, or beat around the bush, so I blurted out, "Angels. It's about angels, Mary. I've seen one or more probably. I've talked to him repeatedly and I know what I know. You can think I'm crazy, or making this whole thing up, but I'm not. What do I have to gain from sounding like a lunatic? There are simply no explanations for what I've seen and heard and I am positive I've had contact with angels. I'm positive, Mary."

Mary didn't say anything at first. She took a drink from her water bottle, then asked, "Is this what you talked to the preacher about?"

"Yes."

"And what did he say? Did he believe you?"

"I've actually had three conversations with Will. I think he was intrigued and very interested in what I was telling him. I think he wanted to believe me."

Mary ran her fingers through her hair, temporarily distracting me, then said, "But . . ."

"But, I arranged a meeting with Will and my angel friend, Joel."

Mary interrupted me and asked, "Your angel has a name?"

"Yes, it's Joel."

Mary nodded, then asked, "Does he have a last name or is he like Cher?"

"Cher has a last name, she just doesn't use it. I don't think Joel has one. I'm not sure angels need last names."

Good old Mary held my stare for a good thirty seconds, then she said, "Jerry, I . . ."

But I interrupted her and announced, "I know you think I'm crazy. I know this sounds absurd and you're wondering what in the world has happened to me. But Mary . . ."

Then she interrupted me and replied, "No, Jerry. I believe you. I truly do. What did Will say when he met Joel?"

"You believe me?"

"Yes. I don't know why you'd lie to me. I truly think you honestly believe you saw an angel. Now, I want to know what Will thought and said when he met your angel."

I knew this wasn't going to be easy to explain. The only way I knew was tell old Mary the truth. I told her how Joel acted like a dancing "Uncle Tom" and put on a display of hoboism that would have convinced anyone that he was definitely not an angel, or probably not even half-way sane. I finished by telling her Will's reaction and his quick exit from the Panera parking lot. Mary kept looking at me and finally said, "I want to meet him, too."

This was not the response I was expecting. I told her that I didn't know how to contact him and I never knew when I would see him—if ever again.

She said, "Well, we'll do it the same way you did with Will. When you see him again, text me, and I'll drive to wherever you are—same thing Will did. I want to see for myself and talk to him. Can you do that for me, Jerry?" She knew, and I knew, I could only say yes.

Mary wanted to brew some hot tea for us. But all this angel talk has left me exhausted, so I begged off and told her I needed to get home and unwind. She walked me to the door and said firmly, "Jerry, text me the very next time you see him, day or night. Do you promise?"

"Yes, I promise." And with that, Mary leaned over and kissed me on the cheek. Suddenly, my thoughts switched from angels and spirits to Mary and her kiss, Mary and her sweatshirts, Mary and her bottom, Mary and how to switch from friendly to naughty with old Mary.

My boss asked me this morning if I'd made a decision yet about transferring to Columbia, S.C. I honestly told him I hadn't had time yet and he was fine. He wants me to tell him by Monday, though. That'll give me the rest of the week and the weekend to think about it. It's a lot of money and I probably won't have this opportunity again. First, I want to get everything tied down here at work this morning and scurry over to Panera for coffee, bagels, and hopefully angels. I'm driving down Reynolda Road at the intersection of Robinhood Road and I catch the red light. I have peanut butter on a hot, toasted bagel on my mind when the light changes and I see someone waiting to walk across the street--- Joel!

I can't stop-- there's too much traffic behind me-- so I pull into the driveway of one of the large, old homes on Reynolda. As soon as I pull in, an older woman is coming down the driveway pulling her garbage can to the curb. She starts saying something to me, but since it's cold outside, I have my windows up and can't hear her. Then she stops pulling the garbage container and starts waving her arms at me. Please lady, just give me a minute!

I see her reach in her coat and pull out what appears to be a cell phone. Holy cow! I quickly back out, not looking, and nearly hit an oncoming truck from Lusk Tree Service. The old lady is still waving at me, talking to someone on her cell phone (probably the police); the old gray-headed man in the truck is blowing his horn at me, and I don't see Joel anywhere. I gun my car, as much as a four cylinder Jeep will gun, and try to get out of everybody's way. I look on both sides of the road, in the rear view mirror, and in front of me---no Joel.

Three more stop lights and a mile and half until the Panera Bread parking lot. I pull in and guess who's standing in front of the store? Yep. This time I don't drop my phone, instead I text Mary immediately, "Panera! Now! Joel!"

I know he wants me to ask him how he got here before me with him on foot and me in a car. But I won't. Instead, I walk up to him and say, "Why did you say I'm not moving anywhere? I'll move if I want to. You can't stop me."

Joel only smiles and says, "Good morning, Jerry. When's Mary gonna get here?"

Ignoring this, I ask again, "Why did you say I'm not moving anywhere? Why? You can't stop me."

"No, Jerry. You're right, I can't stop you. No one can stop you. You and every other person in the world has the freedom of choice. You can do whatever you think you want to do. You can make good decisions and you can make bad ones. You can do the right thing or not. Jerry, you can be smart or you can be dumb. It's all up to you. But, Jerry, you may think you're the only one affected by your choices and decisions-- you're not. That's where I come in."

"What does that mean? Where you come in? I'll move if I want to."

"Okay. Calm down. You can do whatever you want to do. I'm just telling you that you don't know everything like you think you do. Jerry, the privilege of a lifetime is to become who you really are."

I think I'm afraid to ask him this next question: "Okay, Joel...what do I need to know that I don't know?"

Joel looks at me and grins, showing me those perfectly straight, white teeth, and says, "You might not know how your so-called decision to move or not move might affect someone else."

Before I can ask the million dollar question of WHOM it might affect, Mary pulls into the parking lot. We both look at her get out of her car and walk towards us. I haven't introduced them, but Joel says, "Hello, Mary. I've heard a lot about you. Very nice to finally meet you."

Mary looks at me then back at Joel and says, "What have you heard about me?"

I interject myself in this little tete-a-tete and exclaim, "I haven't told him anything about you! I've never even mentioned you to him. I've never even told your name, Mary. You see what I mean?"

Joel smiles, looks back at Mary, and says very reassuringly, "He just doesn't remember everything, Mary. You know how he is. He's quite talkative when he wants to be."

"Okay," Mary says in a firm voice. Looking directly at Joel she asks, "What's your last name, where do you live, and where are you from, Joel?"

Joel smiles and says, "Mary, of all the questions in the world you could ask me, you want to know what my last name is?" But before Mary can comprehend this and decide if that truly is the question she wants to ask him (just in case he IS an angel), Joel answers her: "My last name is Smith. As Jerry's probably told you, I'm quite homeless. And I'm not really from anywhere, Mary. My father was not from any one place; I moved around a lot and I've lived in quite a few places---they all seem like home to me."

At this point, no one spoke. Mary looked at me and I looked at Joel, who just smiled. Then Mary said, "Okay, Joel, tell me the truth—are you an angel or not?"

Hearing this, Joel took his left hand out of his pocket and began unwrapping a bandage from around his palm. It was oozing a little blood and looked pretty bad. He said, "Mary, do you think angels cut their hands and bleed?" He looked at me and laughed a little, then started re-wrapping his hand.

Mary asked, "What happened to your hand?"

Joel picked up his backpack, looked over at the bus just pulling up across the street, and said, "Oh, it was just a little accident, but I've got to get to the clinic and have it checked out. I gotta run now. It was so nice finally meeting you, Mary. You're just like Jerry described you." And with that, he took off at a brisk walk for the waiting bus. Mary stood there gawking at him.

I just shook my head, thinking, not again!

13

MARY LOOKS AT ME and says, "Come by the house after work, I'll make us something to eat. I have to run now." She doesn't even say, "Bye, Jerry." Or whether she believed me or if she thought Joel was an angel or simply some hand-bleeding homeless man making a fool of us. Well, it's just been a great day so far. I started off by infuriating an old woman, then narrowly avoiding backing into a tree service truck. I've been abandoned by Mary and maybe even an angel—if he is an angel. However, coffee and bagels still love me and they will understand.

As I'm trying to decide which bagel I want this morning, I see Ida over at a table talking to some older people. I wait for her to pass near me and I cheerfully say, "Hey, Ida, I'm here again for my daily dose of life sustaining nutrition."

She stops, but doesn't smile, and replies, "Jerry, remember, man does not live by bread alone."

I can't help myself and respond, "I know that, Ida. Sometimes he needs a little peanut butter."

As I'm smiling at my little humorous remark, Ida walks right up to me, without smiling, looks me directly in the eye, and asks, "Jerry, tell me, what is it you plan to do with your one, wild, and precious life?"

I just wanted a bagel and some coffee; I don't want to answer some type of Freudian inquisition into my inner being. That, plus, I don't know how to answer it. Before it becomes too uncomfortable for each of us, she turns and walks away without another word. Now add Ida to the list of people I've displeased this morning.

Even though the weather is cold now, Mary's house is warm inside and she is wearing some loose fitting gym shorts and a tee shirt. When I notice this, I start wondering to myself, "Does she always dress like this or does she only when she knows I'm around?" Obviously, I don't know the answer, but it's fun thinking about it. Mary is preparing a homemade pizza, which smells delicious. As I sit down, she brings me a beer. Mary brings me a beer! No water...a beer. I'm too afraid to formulate the meaning of this. Is it possible old Mary is trying to get me drunk and take advantage of me? A guy can dream.

She starts the conversation, "Well, that was very interesting this morning. First, I'd like to know what you've been telling Joel about me. I don't understand why you'd tell an angel anything personal about me, Jerry. And, if he's not an angel, I'm even more confused about why you'd tell a homeless man about me. Either way, I don't understand. You need to be honest with me if we're going to remain close. The only way to have a friend is to be a friend, Jerry."

"Mary, I told you this morning, and I'll tell you again, I never told Joel anything about you. Not your name, not who you are—nothing! This is what I've been trying to explain to you all along—somehow he knows stuff and I don't understand how he knows that stuff. The only explanation I have is that he's an angel. How in the world could a homeless man know what he knows?"

I take a good long drink from my bottle of beer; Mary drinks from her bottle of water. The pizza is getting cold. She looks at me rather sternly and says, "I don't think he's an angel, Jerry. I just don't believe it. He simply doesn't look like an angel, or act like one...and, he was bleeding for goodness sakes. Angels don't bleed!"

Sometimes I think the most appropriate response is to say nothing, so I don't. I learned a long time ago that women don't want to hear what YOU think. Women want to hear what THEY think—in a deeper voice. But Mary didn't like the silent approach so she continued, "Well...say something, Jerry!"

I know in my mind there is no way out of this. No amount of bralessness is going to save me from further conversations on this subject or make it any more pleasant. I wish everything was as easy as getting fat, but it's not. So, I answer, "Okay, Mary, you say he doesn't look like an angel. Just how does an angel look? How many angels have you seen? And, you say he doesn't act like one either, right? Tell me then, how does an angel act? And what makes you think an angel can't bleed? I imagine if they're angels sent by God, they can darn well do anything they please--- bleed, fly, or disappear! Look, Mary, I'm no genius and I certainly don't know much about religious stuff, but I am smart enough to know that some things I just don't know."

And at this juncture I'm also smart enough to know not to force pieces that don't fit. Obviously, Mary is having a hard time believing Joel is an angel. But deep down, I think she knows the truth.

After a short welcomed pause, we decide to eat some pizza. With our mouths full of mushrooms and peppers (no pepperoni) it is easy for us not to talk about angels any longer. When I finish my beer, Mary brings me a bottle of water. Apparently, I'm on a one beer limit. She finally says, "Jerry, I'm exhausted by all this. I need to go to bed." I was not entirely sure if that is an invitation for me to join her or an invitation for me to leave. I found out when she walked towards her front door and opened it for me.

All this angel business, or not angel business, has prevented me from focusing on one of the most important decisions of my life so far: Do I take the job in Columbia? I have to tell my boss tomorrow of my decision. Logically, I don't see how I can turn down such a big raise and a great opportunity like this. My heart is leaning towards staying here because I am swayed by sweatshirts, bikinis, and lurid thoughts of Mary. Now, I'm not so sure. I think I should probably accept the sure thing and move forward.

Friday morning I tell Art, my boss, that I'll drop by his office about 11:00 and let him know my decision so we could discuss things, either way. I consciously planned this so I would have time to go to Panera and give any angels one last chance to intervene and let me know if I am making a mistake. Joel, nor any other cosmic being, showed up. I eat a blueberry bagel (with peanut butter), have a cup of light roast coffee, and wonder why Ida is purposely avoiding me. She was doing all her assistant manager duties, while never looking in my direction. Finally, I relented and walked outside, waiting for someone—anyone—to walk up to me and say something. Nothing happened.

At 11:00 I go to Art's office to tell him I'd love to accept the job offer and find out when he wants me to report to Columbia. After pleasantries, Art says, "Well, I guess you've come to a decision."

"Yes, sir, I have. I'm going to stay here." No, no no no no no no no no...that's not what I meant to say. I shake my head and say, "No, I'm sorry Art, I didn't mean to say that. I meant to say that I'm staying here." Before I could realize what I'd just said, for the second time,

Art replies, "I don't understand, Jerry. You're staying here, but you didn't mean to say that you're staying here?"

"I'm sorry, Art, I got a little confused. I don't know why I said that. I decided to actually stay here." I SAID IT AGAIN! My mind is trying to digest what's going on here and why I keep saying something I don't mean to say, when the phone rings on Art's desk.

He looks at me and says, "That's Columbia calling, Jerry. I'll tell them you're staying here." He picks up the phone, half turns his back to me, and waves at me as though I should be leaving his office. As I'm still standing there—stunned—I hear Art say, "Yeah, he's staying here. Go ahead and call Bill and make him an offer." He then turns back to me, puts his hand over the phone receiver temporarily and asks, "Is there anything else, Jerry?" I'm still too stunned to respond or move, until his secretary gently touches my arm and nods her head for me to follow her out of the office.

I'm in a daze. What just happened in there? Why did I say something I didn't mean to say...THREE TIMES? Some people I work with knew I was deciding to leave and they had decorated my office and door with signs saying "Bon Voyage" and "We're going to miss you" and had balloons all over my desk. When I walk back they start saying, "We're sure going to miss you, Jerry." "Is today your last day?" "Did Art say who's going to replace you?" I just walk in my office and close the door, still too stunned to actually talk to anyone.

My phone rings and caller ID tells me it's Art. When I answer he says, "Well, Jerry, you sure surprised me a while ago; I thought for sure you'd take that job. But it all worked out in the end. You remember my nephew, Bill, and his wife Gwyn. Well, he just graduated from the university down there and we're going to hire him in that position as a trainee. I'll need you to help him, guide him along, so to speak. But, anyway, it's good to keep you on board here, Jerry. Talk to you later."

The rest of the day passed like I was in a fog. I don't remember much of it and was actually afraid to speak to anyone—I didn't know what would come out of my mouth. Joel! It's got to be Joel. When I get home from work, I call up Mary to see if she wants to get something to eat, or maybe something else. She sounds a little vague and standoffish, then tells me she has plans for the night. This is just not my day. I take a shower and decide to go down to the bar at H&H to see my cousin Joe and relax.

I walk in the side bar at H&H and Joe greets me, while bringing over a cold beer. Since I broke off the engagement with Jennifer, Joe has been very friendly with me. He sets the beer in front of me and asks, "Hey, what are you doing tonight?"

"Nothing," I say, "why?"

He looks to the other end of the bar at a woman sitting by herself, and says, "She just told me she transferred down here from Asheville. I think she said she worked for Wells Fargo. She wanted to know some good places for dinner. Why don't you go over and ask her out?"

I look at the woman, who was attractive in a sultry sort of way, then look back at Joe, and say, "Are you crazy? I can't walk up to a strange woman in a bar and ask her out. She might be married, or involved, or actually have some decent common sense."

"Alright, just thought I'd try to help you out. If you want to continue moping around all your life, go ahead."

"I'm not moping around! I feel good. And, I'm not the kind of guy to just walk up to strange women in bars and start talking to them. Anyway, I think I might start seeing someone soon...someone nice." I could dream thoughts about Mary, but Joe didn't need to know who she was.

He looks at me like he doesn't believe a word I'm saying---and I can't blame him. He leaves me alone so I can think. I wish he hadn't left me alone. I sit and peel the label off my beer, still wondering about my weird conversation with Art this morning. Did I subconsciously say what I did because I really didn't want to leave Winston-Salem? Or, was Joel behind this? I thought angels were supposed to help you, not sabotage your future. As I'm ruminating on this turn of events, Joe comes back over and says, "You're taking her to dinner in twenty minutes. She rode through Old Salem earlier, saw Salem Tavern, and wants to go there. I just called them and they said ya'll can come over now and they'll fit you in."

I'm so flabbergasted I don't know what to say. I look at Joe and he turns toward the woman and smiles while giving her the thumbs up sign. When he does this, she starts walking our way. I quickly whisper to him, "Are you kidding me? What have you done?"

"Shut up, she'll hear you. You'll have fun. Just don't be yourself."

She walks up to us, smiles, and says, "Hi, my name's Danelle. Nice to meet you, Jerry." She has dark brown hair, is a little taller than Mary, wears a lot of makeup, has a nice smile, and looks as though she might struggle with keeping her weight under control—but, I'm not sure about that.

Before I can respond, Joe says, "He loves the Salem Tavern. He's parked down the street. Why don't you just leave your car here, Danelle, and I'll make sure it's okay."

"Great," she says. "Are you ready to go, Jerry?"

Well, apparently, without ever speaking a word to this woman, I now have a date with her and I'm driving us to dinner. With her heels on, she is nearly as tall as me. Before we arrive at the Tavern, she tells me she's just moved here from Asheville and works in the Wells Fargo office in Old Salem. She's only been in Winston-Salem for a week and doesn't really know anyone except the people she works with. She is divorced, after a two year marriage. She does not divulge why she became divorced after only two years.

We have a pleasant dinner, a bottle of wine from Sanders Ridge Winery, and then dessert and coffee. Danelle is the kind of woman that somehow becomes more attractive the longer you look at her. Or maybe it was the wine. No, she is a pretty woman. During dessert, she would be talking to me and her hand would touch my arm when she was telling a story, or making a point. Okay, this is interesting.

When the waiter comes the last time to ask if we want anything else, I look at Danelle, out of courtesy, and she looks back at me, then at the waiter, and says, "No, not here. We might have another glass of wine at my house, though."

Well, we did have another glass or two, or three, of wine at Danelle's rented condo. Then, Danelle proceeded to show me things about sex that I never knew existed—except in porn movies. To say she was ravenous would be a gross understatement. To say I was overmatched would be a rather accurate assumption—but, I tried hard. I really don't know that much about sex, because I've always been with Jennifer.

14

DANELLE ENSURED THE LONG, cold winter nights were anything but cold. After that first night, we saw each other five out of the next seven nights—and, I do mean "saw" all of each other. Danelle was insatiable and the more time we spent together, the more we both loved it. After three weeks she told me she needed to go back to Asheville for the weekend to tie up some loose ends and visit her parents. I volunteered to go with her, but she said she would stay with her parents and it might be awkward if I was there.

Mary had called a few times since I'd been with Danelle, but I didn't return any of her messages. Then on Friday night, after Danelle had gone to Asheville, she called again and I answered the phone—I didn't want to, but I did. "Hey, Jerry. How've you been, I haven't spoken to you in a while. Is everything okay?"

"Yeah, Mary, it's all good. I've been really busy at work." I lied. "How have you been?"

"I'm good, too." A long, uncomfortable period of silence ensued, then, "Jerry, any more angel sightings? Or, talks with Joel?"

So, this is why she's calling me. She wants to know about angels, not about me, and if I am interested in jumping her bones. "No, I guess you were right, Mary. It was all probably a big misunderstanding on my part. I haven't seen Joel, or any other weird beings. I guess he's gone to wherever it is that homeless people go this time of year."

"Jerry, I'm sorry if I said something the last time we talked that made you mad at me. I didn't mean to."

"No, it's okay, Mary. I've just been really busy at work and trying to help my mom out some. You know how it is."

More silence. Then, "Okay, Jerry. I hope we can still do some things together...if you want to."

"Yeah, for sure. That would be great. I'll give you a call and we'll set something up." That's not a lie! I will call her and we will set something up...sometime.

I woke up Saturday morning with a great yearning for a cinnamon/ raisin bagel and a cup of dark roast coffee—maybe two. It's sunny outside as I drive over to Panera, and as I'm scanning the radio I find a station that's playing "Mustang Sally" by Wicked Wilson Pickett, a great tune to sing along with. It would be hard to find a better start to the day! And then I pull into the parking lot and he's standing there. My beautiful day has just turned stormy. His beard seems a little whiter and a little longer since I've seen him. But his smile is the same as I walk up to him.

"Hello, Jerry. Long time, no see."

I could be mean to him, I could ignore him, or just say, "What are you doing here, Joel?"

He gives me this goofy grin and says, "Just kicking down the cobblestones, looking for fun and feeling groovy."

"What?"

He continues, "I got no deeds to do, no promises to keep. I'm dappled and drowsy and ready to sleep. Let the morning time drop all its petals on me. Life, I love you, all is groovy."

Now, thoroughly confused, I ask him, "Are you drunk?"

Then he starts singing, "Slow down, you move to fast,

You got to make the morning last."

I stop him, "Okay, Joel, I get it now."

He says, "I thought you liked old songs from the sixties."

"Why are you here this morning, Joel? I thought you were done with me. You were right. Jennifer was not the girl for me and I didn't take the job in Columbia. What else do you want?"

The grin evaporated from his face and he replied, "I want you to do the right thing, Jerry. That's all. What you're doing now is not the right thing."

In the past I might have been surprised by this revelation, but no longer. In my mind I'm thinking of all the things I could say, all the things I SHOULD say, back to him; however, some things are just not important. Instead, I simply say, "This conversation is over, Joel. Goodbye."

I walk into Panera and leave him on the sidewalk, wondering, whatever it is that angels wonder about. No line again today. I walk up and the young girl taking my order knows me and asks, "Are these together?"

What? I look back at her as she points over my shoulder at Joel who's standing in line behind me. Joel answers her, "Yes, but I'm just having coffee."

How does an angel actually take his coffee? In Joel's case, black. If, in fact, he is an angel...which is the only logical explanation for everything that has happened to me. I do not offer him half of my bagel, even when he looks at it and says, "Wow! That looks good."

Instead, I take a big bite and reply, "It is very good. What do you want, Joel? You didn't come down here to drink coffee and sing me an old song by Joe Cocker."

"Jerry, I'm surprised at you. That wasn't a Joe Cocker song I was singing, it was James Taylor."

I take a sip of coffee, which almost burned my tongue it was so hot, and say, "No, it wasn't James Taylor either; it was Simon and Garfunkel."

Joel smiles again and says, "I know, I was testing you."

I eat the rest of my bagel in silence as we both sip our coffee and look at each other. I finally think to myself that he's probably better at waiting than I am. After all, he has an eternity and I have to get a haircut at 10:30. So I break the silence and ask, "Okay, Joel, what is it you're trying to tell me to do?"

"Jerry, I'm not trying to tell you to do anything. I'm trying to tell you what not to do." And with that statement, Joel rises from the table, picks up his backpack and leaves the restaurant. This has happened to me so often now, I'm not even surprised or bewildered at anything he says. I have a second cup of coffee, mostly to ensure I give him plenty of time to leave before I walk outside. I don't want any more "advice" today.

I don't see him anywhere, and I have an appointment for a haircut, so I finally leave. As I open the door, two scruffy looking teens on skateboards come down the sidewalk. They're not actually supposed to be riding on the sidewalk and I start to say something authoritative to them, but before I do, one of them looks at me at says, "You're making a mistake with that girl, dude."

Really? I hope you hit a crack in the sidewalk and fall. I didn't actually say that...but I wanted to! I've realized now I'll never reach my destination if I stop and throw stones at every dog that barks.

I can't wait for Danelle to get back in town Sunday. I think I'm becoming addicted to her physically-- in a good, wholesome way, I mean. She had texted to tell me she'd be home about 6:00 and invited me to come over around 7:00. She ended the message with, ". . . and don't be late!" Don't worry about that honey.

Mary calls me early Sunday afternoon and asks if I want to hit some tennis balls with her today. Normally, the thoughts of seeing Mary in a tennis skirt, or shorts, would've made that an easy decision for me. Today, however, I have to lie to her and tell her I'd made plans to visit my mother. I'm still unsure if the reason for Mary's call was to actually "see" me, in a good way, or to "see" me as a friend. It's very confusing. Even though Danelle is all I can handle right now, thoughts of Mary still creep in my mind, in a rather unfriendly manner.

Not twenty minutes after the phone call from Mary, my mother does call me. Talk about karma! Today is my dad's birthday and since he's been gone it's hard for mom to get through this day. She wants me to come over for dinner. Dang! "What time, Mom?

"Come over about 7:15; I'll be home from church then. I've got some lasagna I can heat up."

You cannot be serious! 7:15? I should be deep in the throes of passion (or something) with Danelle by 7:15. So I lie to my mom and say, "Mom, I can come earlier, but I've got a business meeting I have to go to tonight. How about 4:00 or 5:00?"

"No, I'm going on a church trip with my Sunday school class and won't be back then. It's okay, Honey, I understand. We'll do it some other time. You go to your meeting and we'll get together soon."

A big sigh of relief comes over me. "Are you sure, Mom? I just really hate to miss this meeting tonight."

"No, Honey. You go to your meeting and we'll set up something for next week sometime. I love you."

"Love you too, Mom. Bye."

Whew! That was close. Mom's lasagna is indeed very good, but I think Danelle may be serving up something much, much better. Then, Mary crosses my mind again. I told her I was going to visit my mom this afternoon. If she rides by my house and sees my car here, that wouldn't be good. I need to go out for a while, just in case. I decide to go to a movie at the mall where Mary would never see my car.

I get my drink and a large popcorn and go to the condiments area--I like a lot of buttered salt on my corn. There is an elderly lady across from me putting hot butter on her popcorn and she looks up at me. I'm sure she's going to tell me that so much salt is not good for me, but instead, she looks at me and says, "You need to go visit your mother, son."

I know this shouldn't surprise me...but it does. I look back at her and say, "What?"

Before she can respond, two little girls run up to her and say, "Let's go, Grandma; the cartoons are coming on!" She looks back at me, but doesn't say anything further. I look around the theater, just to make sure Joel isn't around, but I'm quite alone.

The movie wasn't nearly as good as I hoped it would be, but the popcorn was excellent. When I left the theater, I didn't see the elderly lady, for which I was thankful. I got in my car, grateful not to have any further interaction from strangers, and looking forward to my "date" later tonight.

I pull out on Jonestown Road and catch the red light at the intersection of Country Club Road. As I come to a stop, ready to make a right on red, a bicyclist pulls up, partially blocking me from turning. I roll down the passenger window to yell at him to move, but he speaks instead, "You need to see your mom, NOW!" Then he quickly pedals off, back down Jonestown Road.

The light changes to green and the driver behind me honks his horn to pull me back to reality.

I make it home, but don't remember if I actually stopped at any stop signs or red lights all the way back. Okay, okay, okay. I text Danelle and tell her I'd be a little late tonight, no later than 8:00. She texts back an emoji sad face. I call mom's cell phone and leave a message that I'll drop by about 7:00 for a few minutes before my meeting.

Mom is thrilled to see me and immediately pulls out old picture albums and starts leafing through them. I think she might be somber or start crying over all the pictures of dad through the years, but she is quite the opposite. She is so happy to relive those memories again. Before I realize what has happened, it is 8:10. I tell mom I am late and have to run. She hugs my neck, kisses my cheek, and tells me she loves me. I text Danelle as soon as I get to the car and tell her I am on the way. I just made one woman happy, now it's time for another woman to make me happy---very happy!

15

I DO NOT KNOW where Danelle learned how to do the things she does, but she's earned an A+ in my grading system. If Jennifer had one quarter the passion—no, ten percent of the passion-- that Danelle has, I'd be married now. I finally pull away from Danelle about 11:45, telling her I must get some sleep. I'm totally exhausted when I get home and can't wait to take a shower and get in bed. I see the phone message light blinking and I'm sure Danelle has probably left me an X-rated message to dream about.

I'm wrong. It's the hospital. The message says my mom is there and I need to get to the emergency room as soon as possible. I called back immediately,

"My name is Jerry McRacken. I got a message about my mom in the emergency room. Her name is Doris McRacken. Is she there?"

"Hold please and let me check that name. Yes, they brought her in about 9:30 tonight."

I was frantic. "What's wrong with her? Is she okay?"

"Sir, you need to get down here as soon as you can."

"Alright, I will. But is she okay? Is my mom okay?"

"Sir, that's all I can say. I don't have any further information. You just need to get here."

I know for a fact I did not stop at any red lights or stop signs on the way to the hospital. Fortunately for other drivers, there wasn't much traffic after midnight. When I arrived, they sent a doctor, a guy younger than me, out to speak with me. He was very professional and very nice, but there's just no good way on earth to tell someone that their mother is dead. I asked all the requisite questions: Are you sure? What happened? When? Why?

She had felt dizzy in her recliner and must've known something was happening because she dialed 9-1-1 on her cell phone. When they answered, they didn't hear anything and got no response. They sent a police officer over to check and he could see through the curtains that someone was in a chair, unresponsive to his calls and knocks on the door. He called an ambulance and broke the lock on the door, but he could tell by her color that she was already dead. He felt for a pulse just to verify. The ambulance attendant verified death and they took her to the hospital. They found my name in her contacts list and called me from there, leaving a message. My mom was dead.

The funeral was quite an affair. Nearly everyone from her church was there. Nearly everyone from my office was there. And Jennifer came. Mary came. And Danelle came. Fortunately, all three of them were very nice, very somber, and never mingled with each other. It was a long, unpleasant, sad day. You only bury your mother once in your life—and you're never prepared for it. Joe came back home with me and helped with all the junk that comes up during a funeral. He was great. My boss told me to take all the time I needed. Joe told me to quit, that I didn't need to work any longer. What?

A few days after the funeral I had a meeting with mom's lawyer about her estate. I was the sole heir, but really didn't know much at all about her personal finances. I knew my dad had left her a nice life insurance policy and I knew mom never worried about money issues...but that's all I knew. When I learned that she left me seven million, three hundred thousand dollars, plus the house here, their cottage at Atlantic Beach, and a small stock portfolio---I was stunned!

Joe knew part of it: His dad and my mother were brother and sister, and his dad told him a little about my mom. And...Jennifer knew. Her mother and my mother were great friends through the church and had confided in each other, especially when they thought we might get married. Maybe this was the reason for all the cards and calls I'd been getting from Jennifer since the funeral.

I took a week off from work to try to settle affairs and other things. None of it was pleasant. I even started getting calls from real estate agents "offering" their services to sell mom's house. What a bunch of vultures. Mary called and offered to come over and straighten up mom's house and clean anything that needed cleaning. Dang, Mary's nice. Danelle told me to call her whenever I wanted some company. Dang, Danelle is nice. Jennifer called to ask if I'd been able to settle all mom's financial affairs, and if I needed her help in looking through mom's jewelry to determine the value of things. Boy, Mary and Danelle sure are nice.

Soon, I did fall back into Danelle's embrace. It was too hard to stay away long. I also took up Mary's offer to come over to mom's house and help sort things out. What to give to Goodwill, what I wanted to keep...things like that. Mary wore a pair of old, loose-fitting blue jeans and a tank top when she came over. A tank top! She had to know that wearing a floppy, old tank top, without a bra, was going to be a major distraction to any red-blooded, normal, male human being. She had to know that! Yet, that's what she wore.

You would think that my carnal urges would have been totally satisfied by the never-ending, lustful requirements Danelle demanded from me. But, the thoughts of Mary in a tank top, roaming around the living room, the kitchen, and the bedroom—

even my old boyhood bedroom-- were a little too much to simply ignore. After one afternoon of packing boxes for Goodwill, and having Mary "accidentally" rub against me, I took my mental pictures and daydreams of tank tops over to Danelle's place. She commented on my renewed vigor and physical excitement that evening. She didn't need to know that while my body was satisfying her primal urges, my mind was contemplating tank tops and loose-fitting blue jeans.

I thought I was over Mary. Obviously, I'm not.

Mary invited me over for lunch the next Saturday, which worked out well since I already had plans with Danelle Saturday night. Danelle never asked me over to lunch or dinner...she is acutely aware that anyone who thinks that the way to a man's heart is through his stomach flunked geography.

Mary made us a taco salad with salsa and chips. Water to drink. She volunteered her help with anything else that needed to be done at mom's house, but all that was complete. She offered to help me clean my place since I'd been so busy, but it was fine— as far as I was concerned. She offered to help me write thank you notes for flowers and food during the funeral---which I totally forgot. She offered everything and anything I wanted, except what was underneath her Wake Forest University tee shirt that day. Just before I almost slipped up and said something I know I shouldn't say (about what was underneath that tee shirt), she rescued me by saying, "Oh, I'd better get going soon, Jerry. I've got a tennis match in thirty minutes." I think I may have to go over to Danelle's house early tonight.

The taco salad, though nicely prepared and delicious, did not fulfill my culinary expectations. As Mary set the salad in front of me, I was thinking, "Here I am, just a guy sitting in front of a salad, wishing it was a bagel." Therefore, after my salad appetizer, I was ready for my entrée at Panera when I left Mary's house.

I had not seen or heard from Joel, or any of his minions, since before mom died. I did not miss them. I would not have missed seeing Joel today either, but I didn't have that chance. Here he is. This time I don't even say hello to him, I just pass by him and walk inside Panera. He follows me. The young lady asks me again, "Are these together?"

"No. They are not." I place my order, get my coffee, and walk to an open table. Joel doesn't order anything, he just follows me. I still haven't spoken to him, but he sits down anyway, and says, "I'm really sorry about your mother. She was a fine woman." I nod, wondering how he knows anything at all about my mother, and he continues, "Jerry, you really need to reevaluate your female relationships. It's time you started making some intelligent decisions."

I slammed my coffee cup down, splashing a little on myself in the process, and said, "What in the world are you talking about? Who are you to tell me who I can see and who I can't? If I have 'free will,' like you say, then, by God, I'll see whoever I want to see, whenever I want to see them!"

Joel sat there looking at me, not smiling, not anything—just looking at me. Finally, he says, "And what if your 'free will' decisions hurt a lot of people, Jerry? Are you going to be happy with that?"

"Exactly what are you trying to tell me do then? Why don't you just say it? I'm sick of all this innuendo—just   TELL   ME WHAT I SHOULD DO!"

My raised voice seems to have garnered the attention of everyone on this side of the restaurant. Even Ida comes out from the back room to our table and asks, "Is everything okay here fellas?" Neither one of us takes his gaze off the other. Ida then says, "Jerry, is everything okay, or do I need to call somebody?"

"No, everything is fine, Ida. We just had a disagreement. We're good."

She walks away and Joel says, "Jerry, I've told you before, I cannot tell you what to do—that's your 'free will.' But I can tell you when you're wrong--and you're wrong! Spending all this time with Danelle is not the right thing for you. You know that, don't you?"

I am totally flabbergasted by his statement. I tell him, "I'll see Danelle, or anyone else I want to see, anytime I want to, for as long as I want to."

Joel slowly rises from his seat. He picks up his backpack and says, "Ignorance is bliss, except when it hurts." He walks away and I'm so mad I can't eat my bagel. When he's gone, Ida comes back over to me and says,

"Jerry, if he's bothering you, I can call the police."

"No, we just had a disagreement. He's fine." Then, to change the subject, I look up at Ida and say, "I haven't talked to you lately. Is everything okay with you?"

For a moment I think Ida might start crying, but she recovers and answers, "You've never before asked me how I am."

Before I can answer, even if I knew how to answer, she turns and walks away. I need something I don't have to think about, I need something easy and fun. I need Danelle. We have a date, if that's you call it, for 7:00 tonight, but I need to feel better sooner than that. I throw my cold bagel away and pour out my coffee. I'm going home, take a shower, and go to the one place where I know I'm welcome.

I'm only three hours early, but I know Danelle's home; I see her car in the lot. I park next to her car and look in the rearview mirror to check my hair—I'm a little vain—and I see Danelle's door open. Then I see an older man back out the door, with

Danelle wrapped around him and kissing him very, very passionately. I scrunch down in my seat a little and watch them all but have sex right there in the door way. After he finally leaves, I start up to her place, full of anger, then stop. No. We have no commitment, no promises made, and no understandings. I'm a fool. I get back in my car and drive to the bar where Joe works.

16

FORTUNATELY FOR ME, Joe wasn't very busy yet. Late afternoons are usually the last lull in business before the serious drinkers and partyers start showing up. I probably shouldn't have, but I told Joe what just happened to me at Danelle's house. He took an interest in my story since he's the one who introduced us that day in the bar. His first question to me was, "Did you two have any sort of understanding?"

"No," I answered. "We never discussed anything, we were just having fun, and I thought it would continue."

"Well, why can't it continue? She hasn't told you she wanted to stop seeing you has she?"

"No, she hasn't." This seemed like a logical answer, but I knew it wasn't the answer I wanted. "I just thought she only wanted to be with me. Seeing her with another man changes things for me. I thought she was a good girl, Joe."

Joe shook his head slowly, then said, "She was a good girl wasn't she? Didn't you have fun with her?

"Yes, I did. She was fantastic. But I don't know if I can forget what I saw today."

Joe leaned in close to me and said, "Look knucklehead, you've got a good thing going with her. Don't ruin it by thinking too much. Good girls may go to heaven, but bad girls go everywhere...in your case, places you've never been before and probably won't get to again."

Maybe Joe is right. Now that I know how things are with Danelle, I can just use her to fulfill my sexual fantasies while I wait for a "good girl" to come along. And, who knows—maybe Danelle will change and turn out to be the girl I was waiting for. It could happen. Anyway, I'll still keep my date tonight with her and see where it goes from there.

I have time to get home, change clothes, and still get over to Danelle's place in plenty of time. I'm glad I stopped in to talk with Joe...I think. As I get out of the shower the phone rings again with one of those mystery calls I've been getting. I answer but, as usual, no one speaks and I hang up. As I'm thinking about calling the phone company to have my number changed, the phone rings again. This time someone does speak. Before I even say hello, a man's voice, a voice I've never heard before, says, "Don't go over there tonight. Stop before it's too late." Before I can answer or even ask who's calling, he hangs up. Then, the weirdest part: I immediately hit the recall button and get a recording that says the number is "no longer in service."

Okay, three explanations for this call. First, it's one of Joel's minions. Second, it's the older man I saw coming out of Danelle's place earlier (but how would he know about me and have my phone number?) Or, third, it was a wrong number. Right...who am I kidding?

I pull up in front of Danelle's place and start to open my car door--and I can't. I can't do it. I can't go up there. The thoughts of her being with another man a few hours ago will not leave my mind. This is not what I want. Why can't I find a nice girl, a sexy girl, a girl I truly want to be with...like, Mary?

I pull out of the driveway and start back home, calling Mary on my cell phone as I drive. No answer. I drive by her house and her car is not there. I drive by the church; no one there either. Mary, where are you? As I'm driving aimlessly down University Parkway, my phone rings. It's Danelle. "Hello."

"Jerry, are you running late? Is everything okay?"

Do I lie to her? "Danelle, I'm not coming over. I'm sorry."

Now, I'm bracing for the inquisition: Why? What happened? Will you come over tomorrow? Etc., etc., etc. But instead, all she says is, "Okay. Bye, Jerry."

I wasn't really expecting that. Before I realize what's happening, I find myself in the middle of the small town of Rural Hall. How did I get out here in the middle of nowhere? I turn around and head back downtown to Joe's bar. When I walk in the tavern, Joe starts shaking his head. He brings a beer over to me and asks, "What happened?"

I give him the short version and tell him I just couldn't do it. The sex was great, and I'll miss it, but it just wasn't that important to me. Joe doesn't say anything; he just takes his pen and writes a phone number down on a napkin and hands it to me.

"What's this?" I ask.

He says, "It's the number of a prostitute."

"What?!? Are you kidding me, Joe? I'm not paying anyone for sex!"

Unsmiling, he looks at me and replies, "When a guy goes to a hooker, he's not paying her for SEX. He's paying her to leave."

I drop the napkin, with the phone number, on the bar next to my untouched beer and walk out the door.

For once, I want to see Joel. I want him to be there waiting on me at Panera, but he isn't. I don't even see Ida this morning; I'm left quite alone with my thoughts to enjoy my blueberry bagel and dark roast blend. I silently watch one table of retirees re-living old stories from work. Another table of middle-aged women, obviously not working, are sitting around gossiping about who wore what to the latest Pilates class. Two college girls are sitting across from each other, texting someone else—boyfriend? Girlfriend? Parents? And one lonely looking woman is sitting by herself staring into her coffee cup. I wonder if she's happy, or sad, or exactly what's on her mind. And then there's me—eating a peanut butter covered bagel and drinking a cup of coffee, thinking about angels and a certain braless friend. What an odd combination we all are.

In the weeks after my mom's funeral, Jennifer (my ex-fiancée) was calling and leaving messages daily. I'm sure she just misses me and regrets letting me slip through her fingers. Certainly it has nothing to do with the nearly eight million dollars I've inherited. Even I'm not naïve enough to believe that. Which is why I don't answer her calls or return her messages.

After several weeks Jennifer's calls have all but stopped and her attempts to reconcile with me have faded away. And, aside from a few meaningless phone conversations, Mary and I haven't done anything either. When I've called her, she's not home, I think she must have a boyfriend, or girlfriend—I don't know. I never had any further contact from Danelle, except for a few X-rated dreams. And I haven't seen Joel or had any other unexplained incidents. Just as I'm beginning to think he's disappeared from my life, he shows up. Not at Panera, but at a gas station one morning when I'm filling up my tank. He's standing at the bus stop, in the rain, on the opposite corner looking at me. I finish pumping the gas and notice the city bus pull up to the stop where he's standing. When the bus leaves, he's still standing there, in the rain, looking at me.

I grab my umbrella, lock my car, and walk across the street towards him. "Hello, Joel. It's good to see you again. How've you been?"

"I've been busy Jerry. In fact, I've come to say goodbye. It's time for me to move on; I have other more pressing issues at hand."

Jokingly, I reply, "Was it something I said?"

"No, quite the opposite. It's something I'm going to say."

I look at him rather seriously and ask, "Are you going to finally tell me what it is I'm supposed to do with my life?"

Joel laughs a little and says, "Jerry, my friend, I'll tell you once again, you can do anything you want to do. All the decisions are completely up to you."

"Okay, if that's the case, what is it you came to tell me?"

Joel picks his backpack up and slings it over his shoulder. Then he says, "I'll give you a choice Jerry. I'll tell you what you what you want to know—but that knowledge comes at a great price, one that you might not be willing to pay. Or, I'll simply hop on the next bus and you'll never hear from me again."

I absolutely know that I should not ask this next question, but, how can I not? "What is this great price that I might not be willing to pay?"

Joel looks at me and replies, "Jerry, that price is knowing about your future life. How long you'll live, what you'll know during your life, and most importantly, what you won't know."

How do I answer that? Do I really want to know when I'll die? I don't think so. Or, do I? No...I definitely do not want to know. I'm positive of that. "Okay, tell me." I'm such an idiot. I know I don't want to know and still I can't help myself.

Joel is not grinning any longer. His eyes are set on mine and he starts, "I'm going to tell you what's in your future, Jerry. How it happens, when it happens, and where it happens is all up to you. But have no doubt, my friend. It will happen."

"Okay, tell me."

"You're going to get married at some point, maybe soon, maybe later—totally up to you. And, you're going to have a daughter."

I stop him and ask, just for confirmation, "You're telling me I'm going to have a daughter?"

"Yes, a beautiful little girl, whom you'll be very proud of."

I stop him again and ask, "So, this is the reason for all the stuff that's been happening to me? You wanted to make sure I get married and have a daughter? Why will my daughter be so special?"

"Oh, she won't be, Jerry. Not like you're thinking. Don't get me wrong; she'll be beautiful and smart and a good person. But she's not our purpose."

"Who is your purpose?"

"Jerry, your daughter is going to have a daughter of her own one day—your granddaughter will be the special one. Your granddaughter is the reason we're here, to make sure you're on the right path. To make sure you have the daughter we want. To make sure she has the daughter we need."

"So, my granddaughter is going to be special?"

"Not really, Jerry. I mean, she'll be smart and pretty and a good person, but nothing really out of the ordinary, except she'll marry a man who is special. That's all you need to know. We need your daughter to have a daughter who marries someone special--that's the gist of it."

"How will she know who to marry? Are you going to intervene in her life like you've done in mine?"

"No, we won't have to, Jerry. She'll know—she's going to save his life one day and they'll be bonded together forever."

"What? How will she do that? Can you tell me?"

"Are you sure you want to know, Jerry? It comes with a price."

"Of course I do."

"She'll be a National Park Ranger in Moab, Utah. She loves the outdoors and loves the American west. It is early spring and the area has been hit with a late snowstorm. A rafting company will call the ranger station in Moab one day and tell them they were supposed to pick up a hiker at the confluence of the Green River and Colorado River. When they came down the river and got to the confluence, the hiker was not there and he never showed up. They waited over eight hours, but never saw him.

Your granddaughter goes out to the trail that leads to the confluence and starts hiking it in the snow. After nearly four hours, she finds a man who has slipped off a rock face, broken his leg, and gashed his head. His cell phone has been smashed and he can't walk. He's been out there for nearly thirty-six hours with nothing but some snow to eat. He was supposed to make it to the confluence earlier to meet the rafting party, but his fall prevented that.

Your granddaughter calls for an air ambulance and he is transported to the hospital in Moab, where they set his leg and treat his hypothermia and dehydration. Your granddaughter stays with him and checks on him for several days until he can travel. The man was from Berkeley, California and was a professor at the University of California. He and your granddaughter start a romance there in the hospital and eventually marry. Several years down the road, he develops a cure for pancreatic cancer, which will save countless lives. All because your granddaughter saved his life."

I looked at Joel and ask, "And this is all true? It's all going to happen? My granddaughter is actually going to save this man's life?"

"Yes."

"I can't wait to meet her."

"Jerry, you'll never know her. You'll never see her. That's the price you will pay."

"What does that mean? I don't understand, what does that mean?"

"Jerry, all I'm allowed to say is just that you'll never know her."

As Joel tells me this, another bus is pulling up and the gas station owner is yelling at me to come and move my car. Joel's starting to get on the bus and I urgently ask him, "Who am I supposed to marry for all this to happen?"

He takes one step up on the bus, out of the rain, looks over his shoulder at me, smiles, and says, "You'll know."

17

I'LL KNOW? HOW WILL I KNOW? I'm going to have a daughter with a woman who is unknown to me. Then, she's going to have a daughter, whom I'll never meet. Okay, worst case scenario (for me) is, I impregnate a woman right now and nine months later we have a daughter. Then, maybe eighteen to twenty years later my daughter will have a daughter—whom I'll never see. The absolute worst case is that I impregnate this woman and die tomorrow, my job in this whole affair being finished. I could die tomorrow!

Best case (again, for me) is that I don't marry for a while--or, I do marry but don't have a child for many years. I could still be a father twenty or thirty years from now--maybe more! Then, when my daughter is born, she could wait until she's around forty to have her daughter—all of which means I could live for about seventy more years! So, what has Joel actually told me? I could die tomorrow, or anytime up to seventy years from now. What sort of revelation is that? Any drunk at the county fair could've made that forecast.

My more immediate concern is who will be the mother of my daughter. Will I marry this woman or just have a child with her out of wedlock? Will she be my only daughter? Will I have other children? What, actually, has Joel told me? Answer: NOTHING! Jerry, old boy, ask yourself this question...did you actually see him do anything angelic? Aside from making a few bizarre predictions, what exactly has he done for you to believe anything he said? Will, the preacher, doesn't believe he's an angel, nor does Mary, and she's probably smarter that I am. Well then, little voice in my head, why do I believe him?

Right now, I'm a bit confused. Right now, I don't have a woman in my life. Jennifer and I have definitely broken up, Danelle and I have ceased our wicked ways, and Mary seems to be unavailable all the time. However, I do have a lot of money and Las Vegas is only a few hours away by airplane. I've never been to Vegas; in fact, I've never been west of Tennessee. I doubt I'll find the future mother of my daughter in the City of Sin, but it might be fun trying. Plus, I looked on the map and Vegas is not too awfully far from the little dusty town of Moab and Canyonlands National Park—where the trail to the confluence of the Colorado and Green Rivers is—the place where my granddaughter will save the life of the man who created the cure for pancreatic cancer. If Joel indeed told me the truth. If, indeed, Joel is an angel and not a fortune-telling, dancing hobo.

I find a non-stop flight from Charlotte to Las Vegas that arrives at nearly midnight. I fly regular tourist class because I'm still not used to the idea of being rich. By the time I find my luggage and a taxi it's nearly 1 A.M. but Vegas is totally wide open. Inside the Bellagio, a very nice hotel, I can't tell if it's 1 A.M. or 1 P.M. All the windows are tinted so you can't see outside and there are people everywhere, drinking, gambling, and doing some stuff I can't even recognize.

I don't know anything about gambling, but slot machines seem pretty easy. After checking into the room, I find a machine that takes quarters. Before I've even lost five dollars, a pretty woman comes up to me and takes a drink order. And, the drinks are free! (If you don't count the ten dollars I've lost in slots by now.) I win a little back, then lose a little more, and this pretty woman keeps bringing me drinks—I love Vegas.

After a bit, an older woman sits next to me for a few minutes and the girl brings her a drink as well. It is then that I notice the older woman tipped the girl something. Uh, oh. I didn't realize I was supposed to "tip" for these free drinks. I wait for the bar girl to come around again, then I tip her well and go to my room. I'd lost less than forty dollars in my first night in Las Vegas—I count that as a success.

The next morning I rent a car and get directions to Moab, Utah. It's a lot further than I realized, but I've made my mind up now— I am going to see where my granddaughter will work. It takes me all day to make the drive through the desert wasteland that seems devoid of anything but rocks, sand, and scrubby little trees and bushes. I finally make it into Moab around dusk and find a chain motel room for the night. The room clerk gives me directions out to Canyonlands National Park. I made the eighty minute drive out in the morning and find the trailhead for the confluence overlook.

Mine is the only car in the small, dusty parking lot. I don't know how long the trail is, or anything about it, but I'm in pretty good shape—I'll be fine. I have an orange and a cold bagel from the hotel with me, and I bought a bottle of water from a gas station. All of this I carry in a plastic grocery bag.

Up one slope, down another. I cross a large sandy area, scramble across some rocks, and stop and stare in wonder at rock formations I'd only seen in magazines. Vast mountain ranges in the distance and crevices and boulders up close. I never see another living creature, except a few buzzards circling overhead. I see many, many places where someone could slip and break a leg. I finally make it to the end of the trail after three hours or four hours—I don't really know. But I'm tired. I sit on the edge of a precipice that overlooks the point where the two mighty rivers join.

The Green River, dark and swift, flows from the north and the Colorado, reddish and foamy, from the east. They don't actually merge at all. In fact, they flow together, each river a slightly different shade of color and they flow side by side, almost as if they are somehow separated in the same channel. Certainly, downstream near the rapids, they'll be mixed up into the turmoil that becomes solely the mighty Colorado River--too thick to drink and too thin to plow.

The orange and bagel go very well together. Peanut butter would have been better, but I'll be fine. I run out of water half way back and start getting cold as it gets darker. The trail seems a little different on the way back; there are several views I don't recognize. For the uninitiated, there are no sidewalks or markers. Sometimes it is just a dusty path with a few faded footprints; and over the slickrock itself, there is nothing to guide you but common sense.

It is getting darker quick and I have no idea how far it is to the parking lot. I don't know if I am close or not close and I start to get a little concerned. Just as I scramble down a large boulder I am startled by a young girl with a backpack walking towards me. We both stop and she asks me where I'm going, and I tell her to my car at the trailhead. She looks at me and asks, "Do you mean the trailhead for the confluence overlook?"

"Yes. That's where I left my car."

She nods and says, "I'm sorry sir, but you're on the wrong trail. You must've gotten confused. This trail goes into the Maze— there are no roads there at all. The trail back to the confluence overlook is back about a mile or so. C'mon, I'm going that way. I'll show you the right path to get on."

I turn around and follow her for about an hour, then in complete darkness, she shows me a faint path, lit only by a three quarter moon. I follow her directions and finally make it back to my car with a big sigh of relief---that was scary!

I drive the little winding road out of the park and come to the ranger's station at the entrance where I have to stop for them to open the gate. The ranger tells me his two associates are checking all the lots and roads for me because they had become worried. I apologize to him and tell him I'd have been a whole lot later if the young girl hadn't helped me. The ranger looked at me and said, "What young girl?"

"The girl I met on the trail. She was backpacking and helped me when I got lost."

"There is no one left out here. We've accounted for all visitors in the park. You're the last one. We check everyone in and then we check everyone out. You're the last one." He looks at me as though he wants me to say something. I don't know what to say. Then, he breaks the silence and asks, "Are you sure you saw a girl with a backpack? I can have one of the other rangers go looking for her in the morning."

Knowing my history, I lie to him. "No sir, I think it was much earlier in the day when I actually saw her. I was just a little confused." He looks at me like he doesn't believe a word I've said—and I don't blame him. I'm not a good liar. Before he opens the gate for me, he goes inside the little office and I can hear him calling the other rangers on his radio, but I can't really tell what he is saying. He comes back out and asks if he can get my name and contact information in case they need more details on the girl. I give it to him and they let me pass. I make the drive back to Moab trying really, really hard not to think about what just happened to me back there on the trail from the confluence.

18

I SPENT A TURBULENT and frightful night in my little hotel room in Moab. My mind wouldn't stop racing and thinking. I rose with first light and had a cup of coffee and a peanut butter-less bagel before I started the journey back to Las Vegas. I took a short detour through Arches National Park and saw all sorts of hoodoo rock formations and arches of untold magnificence and sizes. I could now understand why my granddaughter would want to work in this region. Except for the remoteness, the desert, the sand, and the rocks, it was a beautiful place.

I checked back into the Bellagio for my final night in Las Vegas--I figured I could afford to lose forty or fifty more dollars. After a shower and a nice dinner at the buffet, I went back to the slots. I had barely sat down when the same pretty girl from before came and offered me "free drinks" again. I tipped her this time. The third quarter I played won a jackpot of four hundred dollars. My slot machine began blinking with bright lights and a siren was going off. All the other players soon gathered around me to see what I'd done. I accepted congratulations from everyone and felt like a minor celebrity for a few minutes. The drink girl even brought me a drink without me ordering it. Yep, I love Vegas.

I was unsure if I should keep playing or take my winnings and quit. It was only 8:30 at night and my flight home wasn't until tomorrow morning at 11:00. As I sat there pondering this decision, the drink girl came back around and said, "Congratulations. Are you going to keep playing or cash out?"

"I'm not sure. What do you suggest?"

She smiled at me and replied, "I suggest you keep what you won instead of giving it all back—which is what will happen if you continue playing. And then meet me at the bar for a drink, when I'm officially off work in fifteen minutes."

Hoochie mama! I really like Vegas. I told her I'd meet her and she smiled and said, "My name's Ariel. See you in fifteen minutes."

I went to the bar she pointed to and a few minutes later Ariel came around the corner. She had changed out of her "waitress costume" and wore traditional blue jeans and white cotton blouse. When she sat down, I said, "My name's Jerry . . ."

Before I could say anything else, she shocked me saying, "I know your name, Jerry. You shouldn't be here. Go back home. She's waiting for you."

I couldn't believe what I was hearing. "Who's waiting for me? And, how do you know my name?"

Instead of answering either of those questions, she rose from the bar stool, looked at me and said, "Go back home." And she turned and walked around the corner of the bar. Now, I don't know much religious stuff, but I'm pretty sure angels are not drink girls working in casinos. At least I was pretty sure until I went to the bartender and asked him when Ariel came back to work. He didn't know anyone named Ariel. There was one other bar away from the casino. I stopped there as well but they didn't know anyone named Ariel either. I'm changing my mind...I really don't like Vegas.

No more drinks for me. No more slots either. I went to a small club in the hotel where a Bob Dylan impersonator was performing. He sang better than the real Dylan and looked better as well—which wasn't that hard to do. Right now, I just want go home and find out who in the world "she" is.

The flight home was crowded and bumpy. The traffic in Charlotte was a terrible mess—I don't know how people actually live there. But as I drove into Winston-Salem, the clouds parted, the sunshine bounced off the archway over the interstate, the Wachovia building stood erect, the Reynolds Building looked magnificent, and the Innovation Sector was full and bustling with activity. I love my home.

I thought for a while about actually retiring from work. I had enough from the inheritance to live comfortably for the rest of my life—not extravagantly, but comfortably. But then I thought, retire to what? I don't play golf. I don't fish. I don't do much of anything, except work. I sort of enjoy it. If I retired, what would I do every day when I woke up? All day? Every day? Nope, I'll keep working—for a while anyway.

I called Mary when I got back home. Again, no answer. After being gone nearly a week, I only had one message on my answering machine. It was from the preacher, Will Simpson, asking how I was doing. I miss my mom. I miss old Mary—I really miss old Mary. I miss being with Danelle—I don't miss HER, I just miss being with her. And, I sort of miss Jennifer a little bit. No...I'm just feeling sorry for myself now. But I do miss Mary.

Monday morning, back to work, and it feels good—comfortable. After I catch up on everything, I take my morning sabbatical to Panera Bread. My mouth is almost watering in lustful anticipation of a hot, toasted cinnamon/raisin bagel, covered in smooth peanut butter. I may even have hazelnut coffee today...no, I'll have dark roast. I'm not that wild, yet. It's reassuring to know I won't see a homeless, black man, with a white beard and perfect teeth standing outside waiting on me. But, I'm also a little disappointed that I don't find Ida waiting for me. She quit. Ida quit! This ruined my morning. Oh, I still ate the bagel and drank the coffee, but...it wasn't the same. How could Ida do this to me?

After I finished eating, I went back to the counter and learned from the cashier that Ida hadn't actually quit, but had taken a job promotion as the manager of the Panera off Hanes Mall Blvd. I'm not driving all the way over to Hanes Mall Blvd and fight that traffic for a bagel. Ida or no Ida—I'm not doing it.

Tuesday morning I drive over to Hanes Mall Blvd for a bagel. Ida sees me walk in and starts smiling and walking over to me. When she gets close, I say, "Ida, what's going on? How could you move away like that? You didn't even tell me."

The smile quickly disappeared from her face as she replied, "Well, Jerry, I wasn't aware I owed you an explanation for anything I did. I thought I was just the person serving you a bagel every day."

"I didn't come in every day."

"Sorry, Jerry. You're right. But then, you're always right, aren't you?"

"Why are you mad at me, Ida? I'm just curious why you left."

"It was a promotion—okay, Jerry? I'm manager of the store here, more responsibility and more money. Sorry I didn't inform you of the change...I apologize for your inconvenience."

We both stood four feet away, staring at each other, trying to think of what to say next. I was as lost as she was. Then she said, "Go find a seat, I'll have someone bring you your bagel." Ida then turned and walked back into the kitchen area. After a few minutes, a young girl did indeed bring me a fresh, hot, toasted, plain bagel...with cream cheese! Somewhere, back in the depths of Panera's kitchen, I'm sure Ida is smiling.

After work, on the drive home, I tried calling Mary again. I was driving by her house and saw her car in the driveway as I dialed, and she still didn't answer. Hmm. So I ate a frozen pizza, took a shower and decided to go see my cousin Joe at the bar tonight. I might drive by old Mary's house on the way...maybe. Her car was still there, and she didn't answer my call again.

The sidebar at H&H was bustling tonight, but there was an empty space at the bar. Joe saw me and brought me a beer over. We caught up a little, in between him filling drink orders. He wanted to know what I'd done in Vegas, and I know he would've been disappointed in me if I told him all I did was play some quarter slots, so I told him a lie. I told him I played blackjack and won a little at the roulette table and went to a topless show at the hotel. I'm pretty sure he didn't believe any of that.

During my second (and last) beer, Joe asked me if I wanted to meet a woman seated several seats down from me at the bar. I firmly told him "NO!" No more bar women for me. In my mind, I'm quite certain the woman I'm looking for to be the grandmother of my granddaughter is not sitting in a bar on a Tuesday night drinking beer. "Okay," Joe said, "she saw us talking and asked who you were. I'll tell her you're gay."

"Shut up, Joe!"

And then, my cell phone rings. It's Danelle. I rush outside the bar so I can hear better, and Danelle says, "Hey, Jerry. How've you been? I was just thinking about you and thought I'd call."

I try to switch hands and move the phone to my right ear, so I could hear better, and drop the phone. The face cracks but it doesn't disconnect, "Danelle, are you still there?"

"Yes. What was that noise?"

I should've lied to her, but, as you know, I'm no good at lying. "I dropped the phone, the face cracked a little bit."

Danelle replies, "So, my call must've really excited you if it made you drop your phone."

Again, I should've lied to her, but I don't, "Yeah, I guess it did. It's good to hear from you."

"So...would you like to see me as well? All of me?"

Oh, Lordy. Okay little voice in my head, how do I answer this? Tell her "yes" stupid!

"Yes."

"Can you come over? Or, are you busy tonight?"

"No, I'm not busy, I'll be right over."

"Okay. And Jerry...I won't have anything but the radio on."

And she didn't. I'm pretty sure Danelle is not going to be the grandmother of my granddaughter, but she sure can be the devil all men lust for at times in their lives. I did not wonder why Danelle called me after so long, and I didn't care. I knew I was here to serve only one function for each of us...and I am fine with that.

After our second round of carnal experimentation, Danelle got us a glass of wine to sip on while we rested. She eventually told me she had been to the bar and spoken to my cousin, Joe, who told her about my trip to Vegas (and probably about the inheritance). I don't doubt, in the least, that the inheritance news influenced the sudden phone call tonight. I've always found that a duck's opinion of me is largely influenced by whether or not I have bread—it's the same with people.

19

THE PEANUT BUTTER is the only thing keeping me at Panera every day. Since Ida has transferred and Joel has left me, everything seems a little stale now. Oh, I still go, but it would be better if Ida was here to take care of me personally. Now, I just sit here, sip coffee, and either stare out the window at nothing or stare at all the other people sitting around staring at nothing. At least Danelle is keeping my nights filled with excitement—I guess that's the right word. Today, however, I see a familiar face when I walk in...Will, the preacher, is sitting by himself saying a prayer before he eats some sort of healthy looking sandwich.

I wait until he finishes, and before I can say anything, he says, "Jerry, so nice to see you. Can you join me?" I set my tray of peanut butter, bagel and coffee down and notice Will giving it the disdainful look that says, "Are you really going to eat that for breakfast?"

He asks if I want to say a prayer before I eat. Umm, yeah, I guess so. I close my eyes and say my silent prayer: "Dear Lord, thank you for my bagel and give me the wisdom not to say anything too stupid in front of the preacher. And, don't let him find out about Danelle...please!"

Will begins, "How have you been, Jerry? I've thought about you often and wondered about you and your friend, Joel."

"I'm surprised you remembered his name."

"Well, it's not every day you meet someone who might be an angel...is it?"

I'm not quite sure how to answer this question of Will's. Does this mean he might think Joel is an angel? Or does he mean that he only thinks that I think Joel's an angel? I'm thinking too much.

"Will, I was pretty sure you were convinced Joel is NOT an angel. Is that correct?"

The preacher takes a bite of his sandwich and a sip of his tea, sweet tea, for breakfast—and says, "I didn't know, one way or the other, Jerry. At the time, I truly didn't think so. But the more I thought about it, and all the things you told me, I had doubts. As I told you at one of our meetings together, I do believe angels exist and are all around us and that they do intervene to help and guide us. It seems as though Joel may have helped you with some decisions in your life—only you know that for sure. I'll ask you again the same question I asked you before: Do YOU think Joel is an angel?"

"Yes." I say, and I mean it.

Will simply nods and then asks, "Well, have you thought any more about your faith, since you've now been touched by an angel?"

I have not really given that any thought at all, and I shouldn't lie to a preacher—well, not a big lie anyway. So, I quickly come up with what I think is a good response. "I have thought about that, Will. I kept hoping Joel would do some sort of miracle to prove to me he is indeed an angel, then I would definitely believe. But he never did any outright miracles."

Will puts his sweet tea down and says, "Jerry, for the truly faithful, no miracle is necessary. For those who doubt, no miracle is sufficient."

I nod and take a bite of my bagel. Will just keeps staring at me. Finally, he changes the subject and asks what I've been doing to keep myself busy, besides work. Well, I could tell him the truth and describe all the tawdry evenings with Danelle, but I know this was a good time for a little white lie. "Nothing much, just hanging around. Oh, I wanted to ask you if you've seen Mary around lately. I think she might be out of town."

"No, she's definitely here," he answers. "I see her at least a couple of times a week at church. I just saw her last night, as a matter of fact."

Well, isn't that interesting? We finish our breakfast and purposely avoid any more angel talk. Will invites me to come and visit his church, and I promise I will. I wonder to myself if I'm lying again, or do I really mean that? At any rate, we shake hands and promise to keep in touch. He asks me to please let him know if Joel comes back around...he'd like to meet him again.

So, Mary is not out of town. She's just not answering my phone calls...isn't that interesting? I rode by her house again after work today; her car was not there. What do I care? I have a date with Danelle tonight. I guess a night of unbridled, carnal experimentation could be called a date.

I've asked Danelle several times if she wanted to go out to dinner or out for a movie, a ballgame, a drink—anything? She never has. I should wonder if she simply doesn't want to be seen with me in public, or if her desires and needs are all met privately and sexually. I should wonder that—but I don't. I think we're each fulfilling a latent need the other has at this point in our lives. I don't ask what she does on nights we're not together and she doesn't ask me. We have a sexually gratifying, yet emotionally void relationship.

What was it Dickens wrote: "It was the best of times, it was the worst of times, it was the age of wisdom, it was the age of foolishness, it was the epoch of belief, it was the epoch of incredulity, it was the season of Light, it was the season of

Darkness, it was the spring of hope, it was the winter of despair, we had everything before us, we had nothing before us . . ." Yes, Chuck, I know how you feel.

Monday morning, I drive over to Panera to consummate my yearning, weakness, and demand for my daily fix. The woman next in line is driving me and the cashier crazy: "Is that sandwich gluten free?" "Is the steak sandwich from grass-fed cows?" "Which bagel has the lowest calorie count?" "Is your coffee from Columbian beans?" This woman was definitely not an angel, however, she could absolutely be from...well, you know.

When she finally finishes, I truly felt sorry for the Hispanic guy taking her order. Until I order my usual--blueberry bagel, extra toasted, with peanut butter and a small coffee--and he tells me they don't have any peanut butter.

"Do you want cream cheese instead?"

"No, I don't want cream cheese. I want peanut butter."

"We no have peanut butter, sir. I can get you cream cheese."

I'm trying to control my temper. I'm trying to be nice! "I don't want cream cheese, I want peanut butter. Can I please speak to the manager or the assistant manager?"

He smiles politely and replies, "I am the assistant manager, sir. The manager is no here yet."

"Ida always had peanut butter here. Are you sure you're out?"

"I not know who Ida is, sir. But we no have peanut butter. Do you want cream cheese instead?"

Alright, count to ten, or something stupid like that. Just don't speak now. It's only a bad day, it's not a bad life. So, I choose to

NOT take a peanut butter-less bagel, or a coffee; instead, I simply turn around to walk out—quietly and politely.

Then he says, "That'll be four dollars and thirty-six cents, sir."

Everything after that is a blur. The only two things I'm sure of are that my shirt has a coffee stain which will never come out and that I'm banned from Panera.

I am NOT driving all the way across town to the other Panera, in all that mall traffic, just to have some peanut butter. I'll not do it!

Even though it's fairly warm outside, I put on a light jacket and zip it up to cover the coffee stain on my shirt as I walk in the Panera across town. I'm such a liar. Ida sees me right away and comes over to me saying, "What happened? I just got an email about you. I'm not supposed to accept your credit card or serve you."

"Ida, you won't believe what just happened. They did not have any peanut butter and then they kicked me out! Incredible! Can't you come back over there?"

"No, Jerry. I work here now; I'm not going back. Go get your coffee. I'll get you a bagel and peanut butter."

"But, Ida . . ."

"JERRY, GET YOUR COFFEE AND SIT DOWN!"

I get my coffee and sit down. Ida comes over a few minutes later with a cinnamon/raisin bagel and cup of peanut butter. She says, "Butter it up and tell me what happened." I tell her everything (that I can remember). I tell her she has to come back. I tell her they ran out of peanut butter—she would've never done that.

She nods and says, "So you want me to give up my manager's job here, to go back over there, so they won't run out of peanut butter again. Is that right, Jerry?"

Well...it doesn't sound quite right when she puts it that way, but, I have to be honest. "Yes."

Ida rises from the table, picks up my tray (with the bagel and peanut butter), grabs my coffee cup, and says, "Get out, Jerry. And don't come back." Before I can speak, she dumps everything in the trash can and walks back into the kitchen. Women! I'll never understand them.

20

CAN SEX BE BORING? That's the interesting question I've been asking myself lately. Maybe boring is the wrong adjective. Certainly my evenings with Danelle are anything but boring; however, there's definitely something missing. We never go out and we never really talk about anything, except which boring wine bottle to open. I want more. I want a friend and a lover. Mary...what happened?

I've stopped called her because it's apparent she doesn't want to speak to me. Why? I'm not exactly sure. The only time I've actually seen old Mary was one day when I rode by her house and saw her pulling the trash container out to the curb. She looked away quickly and I felt embarrassed that she saw me. It had become a habit for me to drive by her house, more out of nostalgia than of anticipation.

As I'm preparing to leave for Danelle's place tonight, the phone rings. I can see from caller ID that it's Mary. I let it ring three times so she won't think I'm too anxious to answer. "Hello."

"Hello, Jerry. it's Mary."

"Mary...I was wondering if I'd ever see you again. I've tried calling several times."

"I know you have. I'm sorry. I needed time for you to be away from me." I don't really understand what she means by this. She continues, "I needed to make sure you and Jennifer were truly broken up. I'd hate for anyone to think I had anything to do with your breakup. Or played a role in you getting back together. I just felt awkward about the whole thing."

"Mary, you played no role in us calling off the marriage. She wasn't the girl for me, and I'm quite certain I was not the man she was looking for. I'm just glad we figured that out before we married."

A moment of two of silence, then Mary says, "I was getting ready to cook a pizza and I remembered how much you enjoyed my pizza. Do you want to come over for dinner?"

I almost asked her to repeat that question, just to make sure I heard her correctly. "Yes, I'd love to. What time?"

"Come on over now if you want to. I'll heat up the oven."

"Great! I'll be there shortly. And, Mary...thanks."

Oh, crap. What about Danelle? I'm supposed to be at her house in about fifteen minutes. How in the world am I going to explain this? How do I rationalize the decision to eat a pizza (with ingredients I don't really like) rather than indulge in man's primal desires with a woman exhibiting no inhibitions?

Easy...I'll lie to her. "Danelle, it's me. I have some bad news. I ate some fish for lunch today and now I'm throwing up. Every time I try to get out of bed, I get sick. I feel terrible."

"No problem, Jerry. Hope you feel better. Talk to you later." Click. Click?? Well, not exactly the response I imagined—but okay.

Mary is on her front porch when I get there. She meets me at my car and says, "Jerry, disaster! I had some leftovers in the oven and forgot about them when I turned on the oven to preheat it. I jumped in the shower and when I got out the entire kitchen was in smoke."

I heard something about leftovers and smoke, but was too distracted by the Kansas City Royals tee shirt Mary has on to comprehend the meaning of anything she is telling me. Well, not exactly the tee shirt—but, you know what I mean.

She says, "The house needs to air out. How'd you like to go get some Mexican?"

"Sounds great to me. Are you sure your house is okay?"

"Yeah, I turned everything off and left the windows open. It'll be fine in a couple of hours."

We drove to Senor Bravo's, but there was a line at the door. Then we went to Monterrey, but they were closed for remodeling. We weren't worried; there are about a hundred Mexican restaurants in Winston-Salem. Then Mary says, "Let's go to that new place on Liberty Street, Crafted. I heard they have great tacos there." I'd never heard of Crafted, but anyplace with Mary is better than anyplace without Mary. Does that make sense?

We made it to Liberty Street, which is a testament to my driving skills while being utterly distracted, and walked into the restaurant. The hostess took us right back and sat us at a table near the rear. I sat down and looked up at the table across from us, right into the face of Danelle. She was sitting with the same older guy I'd seen her making out with that night in her doorway. She looked at me and did not smile, or say anything, or avert her stare from me. I could feel the x-rays coming out of her eyes penetrating into my brain.

Of all the Mexican restaurants in town, how in the world did we both end up at the same place at the same time? If I didn't know better, I'd swear Joel had to be involved in this somehow. Mary talked, Danelle stared, and I sweated through my shirt. Not even the eight dollar crafted beer I had could cool me off. Somehow, Mary never suspected anything—I don't know why. And Danelle's date was too busy rubbing her leg beneath the table to be aware of anything else. It was definitely the worst dinner I'd ever had.

Danelle and her "date" finished before us, and when they left, she "accidentally" bumped into me as she was passing by. She didn't say "Excuse me," or anything else.

Mary commented, "How rude was that?"

"Yeah, some people!" I replied, while wiping the sweat off my face.

After the dark cloud left, the sun shone in the restaurant. At least it seemed that way. Mary talked and talked about everything and about nothing—I loved it. As I sipped my eight dollar beer and Mary drank from her glass of water (with lemon), I sat there oblivious to everything else around us and gazed into Mary's eyes, thinking, "This has to be the woman who will be the grandmother to my granddaughter." This is the reason for all the "occurrences," this is the reason I was spared in the car accident, this is the reason Joel hounded me. To ensure I got together with Mary. Joel, I forgive you for all the things I thought about you. You're a good, old angel--if indeed you are an angel.

Back at Mary's house, she got us each a bottle of water and we sat around and talked about everything Mary found interesting: the environment, politics, women's rights, global warming, immigration, and several other less stressful issues. She never really asked me how I felt about any of these ideas, which was probably good since I was, more or less, preoccupied with two rather interesting topics hidden underneath a most un-political Kansas City Royals tee shirt. The environment, or Mary? Politics, or Mary's tee shirt? Immigration, or what's underneath Mary's tee shirt? For men, the answer is usually pretty simple.

Old Mary hinted that she probably needed to get some sleep, so I shuffled towards the door, wondering if tonight should be the night when I finally kiss Mary goodnight. I found out quickly that it was not the time for a goodnight kiss. I opened the door and Mary stuck her hand out and said, "Thanks for a great evening, Jerry. I've really missed our friendship. We're good again aren't we?"

Rather than trying to force a denouement of these comments, I simply reply, "Yeah, we're great." On the drive back home, I start wondering what old Mary meant by saying, ". . . our friendship." I have a nagging feeling that my idea of our "friendship" and Mary's idea of our "friendship" may not exactly be the same.

Mary invited me over another night during the week to watch an old movie—a favorite of hers, Dances With Wolves. She really seems to be interested in the west, which would make sense since our granddaughter to be will also love the west and eventually live out there. We watched the movie, me sitting on the couch and Mary sitting on the floor, and drank our bottled water while munching on unsalted popcorn. At the end of the night, Mary gave me a hug at the door. I was hoping for an opening to kiss her, but she pulled away quickly and said, "Thanks for coming, Jerry. Call me tomorrow and we'll plan something for the weekend."

If Joel hadn't been so convincing, I would be finding it very difficult to believe old Mary is ever going to be anything but a "friend," rather than the grandmother to my granddaughter. The little voice in my head assures me, "Just be patient, Jerry. Old Mary's worth the wait, don't screw it up!" Okay, I'll do my best, but Mary could help out a little and wear a bra from to time. She's making it very difficult for me to be patient.

The next morning I went to three places that had bagels, but none had peanut butter. I finally settled on some sort of sissy pastry and a cup of stale coffee from an over-priced coffee shop downtown, which had just re-opened after closing for several months. It should've stayed closed. As I sit in the office reviewing some invoices, it dawns on me that Ida didn't really BAN me from her Panera; she just said to "get out" that particular day. I'm sure it'll be okay to go back there now. Ida likes me.

"You can't come in here, sir."

"What? Why not?" I ask the young hipster, wearing the Panera uniform. He looks back towards the kitchen area and I see Ida back there shaking her head from side to side.

"You're banned from the store, sir. You need to leave now."

I cannot believe this is happening. I ask the hipster to please go back to the kitchen and verify this with Ida, saying, "Just tell her I apologize. We're friends."

He walks to the kitchen and comes back rather quickly, and tells me, "She said you have to leave. And, to quote her, she also said, 'Don't make us call the police.' That's her words, sir."

As I stand here fuming, a sudden revelation comes over me: Jerry old boy, great things can happen today if only I choose not to be a miserable cow. So, I mind my tongue and walk out with my dignity intact and my stomach empty.

21

I CALL MARY and we make arrangements for a double date this weekend: Saturday night, we're going to a dance concert given by the N.C. School of the Arts, and Sunday, Mary invited me to come to church with her. I'm wondering if that means she wants me to spend Saturday night with her. Hmm.

The dance was very good, mixing modern dance with more traditional ballet. Mary loved it. We stopped by Finnegan's Wake afterwards where Mary shocked me and ordered a glass of wine. This must be an omen for what's to come later tonight. When we get back to her house, she doesn't invite me in, but being the gentleman I am, I walk her up to her porch. She unlocks the door and turns to say something, but I surprise her with a kiss instead. She pulls back immediately and says, "Jerry, what are you doing?"

"I thought...well, I thought you would like it. Isn't it time in our relationship for us to kiss?"

Mary had the most quizzical look on her face before she replied, "Jerry, I'm gay. Don't you know that?"

I think I said something, I'm not sure. Then, Mary spoke again, "Jerry, you're my friend, one of my best friends, but I'm in a relationship right now."

Still, fairly stunned, I reply, "A relationship?"

"Yes, my girlfriend is in the Army and she's deployed in Afghanistan right now. She's got another four months until she gets home."

I know I should have been more suave and sophisticated, but, all I could say was, "Girlfriend?"

"Yes. I'm sorry, Jerry. I truly thought you knew. I never meant to mislead you. I simply enjoyed spending time with you—as friends."

"I did too. I mean...I don't know what I mean, Mary. I guess I'm surprised. I'm sorry."

"Jerry, please don't let this change things with our friendship, okay?"

"No, no it won't, Mary." I lied, "We'll still do stuff together."

Mary went inside her home; I got in my car and didn't know what to do. Joel has obviously lied to me, which proves he is definitely not an angel. How could I be so gullible? I head back downtown to the sidebar at H & H to talk with my cousin Joe, but he's off tonight. I order an Iron Maiden. I need something a little stronger than a beer but a little less than cocaine to help me process what just happened. Mary is gay. She will not be the grandmother to my granddaughter...wait a minute! If this whole thing with Mary is a lie, then the entire bizarre story of my granddaughter saving some guy's life is a lie as well. I'm a fool! I let a dancing, singing hobo take me for a ride.

I'm sitting here sipping an Iron Maiden, thinking about Mary and her girlfriend, staring at myself in the mirror behind the bar, when someone taps me on the shoulder. "Is this seat taken?" I know that voice—but I don't know the well-dressed Black man who asked me the question.

I say, "No, feel free." And I turn back around to look at my sorrowful self in the mirror. He sits beside me at the bar and I notice in the mirror that he's sitting there staring at me.

I half turn towards him and he says, "Hello, Jerry."

I know that I know that voice; but I don't recognize him. So, I say, "Do I know you?"

He smiles, showing perfectly straight, white teeth—JOEL! I didn't recognize him because he's clean shaven now. His scraggly beard has been shaved and he has a neat, close-cropped hair cut—and he's dressed very nicely. But, it's definitely Joel. Still smiling, he says, "How are you, Jerry?"

Okay, three options here, as I see it. First, punch him in the nose and walk away, feeling much better. Second, call him a lying hobo and punch him in the nose, feeling much, much better. Or, third, ignore him completely and don't let him wiggle himself back into my life. Before I can decide (and I'm leaning towards option two) he says, "Jerry, I never lied to you. I've always told you the truth. I think you know that."

"Oh, really? Never lied to me? Well just how am I supposed to have a daughter who has a daughter with a woman who's gay?"

He looks at me and says, "Who's gay?"

"Who do you think? Mary, the woman you told me was going to have our daughter, who'd then have our granddaughter. The woman you've been steering me towards. If you're who you say you are, how in the world could you get things so wrong?"

He looked at me, then quit smiling and said, "Mary's gay? Are you sure?"

"Well, she told me herself...so, yes, I'm sure!"

He started scratching his head and replies, "Wow, that really surprises me. I had no idea."

I'm getting madder by the moment, "Shouldn't you know more about the woman you're trying to hook me up with? You must have really flunked something important in angel school."

Joel starts smiling again and says, "So, you actually do think I'm an angel, huh, Jerry?"

"Not anymore. A real angel wouldn't have made the mistakes you've made...that's for sure!"

Still smiling, Joel says, "And just what mistake would that be, Jerry?"

My voice is starting to raise a little too much now, "What mistake? How about Mary? How about me and Mary? How about Mary being gay? How's that?"

At this point, nearly everyone at the bar is looking at us. Joel turns both ways, looks all around us, then says to the bartender, "Everything's okay, we're just discussing something."

The bartender says, "Alright fellas, just hold it down a little. But I'd like to meet this Mary you're talking about."

Everyone settles back to their drinks, and I pick mine up to take a sip, but it's empty. It wasn't empty before...but, it's empty now. I look at Joel and before I can accuse him of anything, he says, "I never told you Mary was the one. I only told you the others weren't the one." At that point in time, as noisy as that bar was, I didn't hear a single sound, except the silence of my heart beating in my chest.

After a suitable time of recovery (one minute, two minutes, five minutes??) I looked back at Joel and said, "Well, who is the one?"

He rose, patted me on the arm, and said, "Like I've always told you, Jerry...you'll know."

He walked out of the bar and got into a cab that had just pulled up. How did a cab happen to pull up at that precise moment in time? What happened to my drink? And, if Mary is not the one...then, who is?

Sunday morning my phone rings; it is Mary calling about going to church with her. Well, after last night, I really don't feel comfortable quite yet. I'll just let it ring and go to Panera...nope, can't go there. I'll go to Krankies Coffee Shop downtown. They probably don't have bagels, but at least it'll get me out of the house. I was right, no bagels, but a wide variety of pastries and some nice smelling coffee. I select a blueberry scone and a medium blend, and find a table near a wall so I can watch all the other people in here watching me. Wall tables are the most popular because they're the ones near plug-ins.

I'm trying to decide whether I want anything else when, much to my surprise, you know who walks in, dressed in a three-piece suit. He walks over to me and says, "Mind if join you, Jerry?"

"Do I have a choice, Joel?"

"Jerry, I've always told you every choice you'll ever make is yours and yours alone. I simply want to give you every opportunity to make the 'right' choice." Joel sits down and we stare at each other for a few moments, then he says, "What?"

Now is as good a time as any to put him to the test. If he is indeed an angel, then there are certain things I want to ask him—things he should know. But before I can say anything, he says, "Go ahead, and ask anything you want."

Okay, I'm thinking...here we go, "Who really killed JFK?"

"Jerry, Jerry, Jerry...I cannot believe, of all the questions in the world that directly affect you, that you choose some inconsequential issue like that as your first question. I'm totally disappointed in you."

"Why do you say it's inconsequential? It was one of the most defining moments in world history?"

Joel nods, then smiles a little, and answers, "Jerry, why does something that happened in the last century have any bearing on what's happening today? Everyone associated with that event is dead anyway. It's best not to dredge up those wounds."

"Well, you're the one who said to ask anything I want. So I did, and now you won't even answer the first question I asked."

Joel looks at me, unsmiling, and says, "Okay, Jerry. A professional assassin named Roberto Barrios made the actual kill shot. Lee Harvey Oswald was indeed a patsy, just as he said. They couldn't let him live after that, so he was sacrificed in order that all the others were protected. Oswald thought, incorrectly and naively, that he was safe. When, after all, he was just a pawn in the bigger picture. You wanted to know who did it, now you know. What good is it to you? Who's going to believe you? Does it make you feel any better, Jerry?"

No, it didn't make me feel any better, but I'll never tell Joel that. Well, I'm figuring now that Joel has to be an actual angel, so obviously, God does exist, but what about heaven. "Second question, is heaven a real place?"

Joel started smiling again as he replies, "Of course heaven's a real place, Jerry. I guess you've never actually read the Bible, huh? It's mentioned several times as being a real place with streets and all sorts of things. Even Jesus told you that He was going to prepare a 'place' for you. It's real, Jerry. Trust me."

"If it's a real place, will I be able to eat a bagel in heaven? Or, play tennis?"

Joel's smile turns into a laugh, then he answers, "Jerry, my friend, if eating a bagel or playing tennis is what it takes to make you happy in heaven, then, yes, you will have a bagel and play tennis in heaven."

"Okay, two more. Is what you told me about what's going to happen with my granddaughter true? All of it?"

"Of course it is, Jerry. I've never lied to you. I'm incapable of it."

"Okay then, last question...who am I going to marry?"

Joel takes a few moments to stare very hard at me—enough to make me squirm—then, he says, "Jerry, you're going to marry the love of your life. The only woman who loves you like you love her. The woman who will make your dreams come true. Now, I'm going to tell you who that is, then I'm going to leave. Are you sure you want to know?"

"Tell me."

Joel rises from the table, smiles brightly at me, showing off his perfectly straight white teeth, and says, "Ida."

22

"DUDE, ARE YOU GOING to clean that up?"

"Huh? What?" I looked up from the table at some millennial, or generation x-er, or maybe just an average tattooed dork, who was looking down at me and pointing towards the floor. I looked down and realized I'd spilled my coffee all over the table and the floor. "Yeah, sorry, I'll get it cleaned up."

I found some napkins and started sopping up the mess. A young girl, with purple streaks in her hair came to help me, and said, "Don't worry about him, he's a jerk!" I truly wasn't worried about him. But he must not have been too much of a jerk, because after we cleaned up the mess she walked out the front door holding his hand. Whereas, I could do nothing but sit down and think...Ida?

Mary called me several times Sunday afternoon, but...no, I can't talk to her right now. Not because she told me she's a lesbian. I'm fine with that—a little disappointed maybe, but I'm fine. I can't talk because of what Joel told me about Ida. I'm going to marry Ida? Ida is the girl of my dreams? Ida is the love of my life? Ida? Really?? I don't understand any of this. Joel is an angel, so he should know. Right?

Okay, Jerry, think! Joel told you about somebody named Roberto Barrios shooting JFK. He could've made that up...easily. Everything he told me about heaven is in the Bible—I checked it out on Google, so no revelations there. I haven't actually seen him perform any miracles; however, I'm not really sure angels actually do perform miracles. If he's not an angel, why does he keep turning up in my life? And...Ida? Is he serious?

Let me think. Ida, what do I know about her? I've only seen her at Panera, in her uniform, which is a somewhat clumsy, loose-fitting, generic pants and shirt, with a cap. I'm not even sure what color her hair is—maybe mousy brown. Her eyes are...I have no idea. Brown maybe. I've never seen her in a dress. I don't think she's overweight. She's probably 5'4" or maybe 5'7" tall, I don't really know. I don't even know her last name! And this is the woman that will make my dreams come true?

Monday morning, after I get caught up with emails and messages, I drive over to the Panera across town, near Hanes Mall—where Ida now works. Why? I don't know. Maybe I'll see her in a different light. At least I'll look at her differently now...I think. I walk in the front door and the Hispanic Assistant Manager sees me and quickly walks back into the kitchen area. Five seconds later, he and Ida come out and start walking over to me. Ida says, "Jerry, you have to leave. You can't come in here."

"Ida, I didn't come here to eat or buy anything . . ."

"It doesn't matter, Jerry. You have to leave—now."

"Ida, I just want to talk to you a minute." I think her face softened a bit hearing this. She turns to her assistant manager and says, "Pedro, call the police."

Pedro looks at me, then back at Ida and says, "Okay, I call police."

"Ida, you don't have to call the police. I'm not here to cause trouble. I just want to talk with you."

She keeps staring at me and says, "Are you calling them, Pedro?"

"Yes, Miss Ida, I call."

She looks back at me and says, "Get out, Jerry. Leave before the cops get here; save yourself some trouble."

"Ida." I'm pleading.

She points at the door and says, "Now, Jerry."

Pedro smiles at me, all the other customers are taking cell phone pictures or videos of me. I guess I'll be on YouTube, or Snapchat, or whatever else that crap is called, hopefully not the 6:00 news tonight. So I leave. Yeah, Joel, this is really the love of my life, alright.

I can't sit at home. I decide to go down to H & H and talk to my cousin Joe and maybe enjoy a beer or two. I would never attempt to explain all this to Joe, or anyone else for that matter. Who would believe me? I'm not even sure I believe me. The bar is only about a third full on this non-weekend night and Joe isn't even here. The bartender with plugs in his ears is working. Not plugs that block sound, but plugs inserted in his earlobes...a trend I totally do not understand. I take a seat at the bar and watch all the other people in the mirror. The college kids haven't arrived yet, too early for them. Just a few people off work and looking to unwind before going home

Then Danelle walks in the bar with a banker-type guy, wearing a three piece black or navy blue suit—I can't tell. But I can tell he's wearing light brown loafers (penny loafers, mind you) with his dark suit. I'm so intrigued by this apparent incongruity that I don't actually hear Danelle speak to me. She waves her arm at me and again speaks, "Jerry, are you okay?"

"Yes. Hey, Danelle. Good to see you." Well, it was good to see her. I think she's lost some weight, or the dress she is wearing is extremely flattering. Either way, she looks good—in a sexy way.

"This is my boss, Clarence Carter...not the singer. Clarence, this is an old friend of mine, Jerry...Oh me, it seems I've forgotten your last name, Jerry."

"McRacken...Jerry McRacken. Nice to meet you, Clarence."

They go to a table about fifteen feet away from me, but Danelle arranges to sit where she's facing the bar where I am. My back is to her but I can see her looking at me in the mirror. Each time I look up in the mirror, she's looking at me. At first, I think I'm a little embarrassed by this whole episode. But now, I realize it's not embarrassment I'm feeling, it's lust and a bit of envy. Danelle is looking good!

We play this "mirror" game with each other for about thirty minutes, then Danelle excuses herself to visit the restroom. On her return, she passes by me at the bar and discretely drops a note next to me. When she is safely back at her table, I unfold the note, which has her lip imprints at the top (done with passionate red lipstick) and reads, "If you still want me, I'll be home after 9:00.

X X X"

I know full well what "X X X" refers to. I miss "X X X." I want more "X X X." The next time I catch her gaze in the mirror, I nod at her and she smiles. The deal is done. There will be multiple "X X X's" in my future tonight.

I don't call her, I just show up at her door about 9:20. She has indeed lost some weight—not a lot—but enough. How do I know? Because she was wearing nothing but high heels when she opened the door. Everything I can imagine is real. Danelle is proof that no matter what people tell you, you don't have to stay within the lines.

I stayed all night and in the morning called in sick at work. Danelle made coffee, took a shower, dressed, and went to her bank job as if it was a normal occurrence. It was not a normal occurrence for me. As I was driving home, a thought came to me: "Jerry, you cannot start the next chapter in your life if you keep re-reading the last one."

Instead of going home, I'd really love to get a hot toasted bagel, with—well, you know what I want. How long am I going to be banned from Panera? Instead, I try a new coffee shop that I saw across the street from Crafted, the taco restaurant Mary and I went to. It's called Liberty Arts Coffee House and it's pretty nice: good coffee, pastries, and even bagels—but only cream cheese. What is this fascination with cream cheese? When I ask the waitress (who had piercings in her ears, nose, eyebrows, tongue, and lips) if they have peanut butter, she looks at me like I'm Gomer Pyle. "No!" she says. "Don't you want cream cheese?"

Having truly learned my lesson, I simply reply, "No thank you, plain is fine." It isn't fine, but I don't want to extend my banishment to this place as well. The coffee is good and the scenery is interesting, as I eat my plain bagel and re-live the licentious and lascivious events of last night. I can't keep my mind from wandering and making crazy comparisons:

Danelle—sexy and sensuous; Ida—plain and unembellished

Danelle—uninhibited and unrestrained; Ida—austere and sober

Danelle—voluptuous and pleasure-seeking; Ida—moderate and straight forward

Danelle--French pastry; Ida—plain white bread

Alright, enough of this! I get a refill of coffee, which is very good, and watch traffic flow by on Liberty Street. My mind has finally stopped thinking and I'm simply enjoying not being at work, when someone taps me on the arm, "Excuse me, but do we know each other?"

146

I turn and see an attractive woman, maybe six to eight years older than me, dressed in a business suit, and holding a briefcase and a cup of coffee. "I don't think so," I reply. "I'm pretty sure I would remember meeting you." I meant that as a compliment, not a come-on.

"I think we met at a conference or gathering somewhere," she says. "What sort of business are you in?"

It seems as though she is uncomfortable holding her briefcase and the cup of coffee, so I ask her to sit down, if she has the time. When she does sit and I can look more directly at her face, she does seem familiar, but not recognizable. I told her where I worked and we made some general inquiries of each other. She said she was here on business, and not from Winston-Salem. Oddly enough, we never asked each other's name or volunteered our own name.

After a moment of silence, she says, "You know, once you stop chasing the wrong things, the right ones catch you." I'm not exactly sure if she was indeed talking to me or was referring to herself. At any rate, I don't comment. We both sip our coffee and watch traffic go by. Then she speaks again: "Jerry, your time is limited, so don't waste it living someone else's life."

I look directly into her eyes, but she is better at staring than I am. I look down at my coffee, then back at her and say, "Excuse me?"

She stands up, picks up her coffee cup and says, "If you're waiting for a sign, Jerry, this is it. Don't be afraid of being different; be afraid of being the same as everyone else. Life is a one-time offer, use it well." Then, she turns, throws her coffee cup in the trash can, and walks out the door.

I watch her walk towards the small city park down the street when I realize she doesn't have her briefcase with her. I look down to get it to take it to her—but it's not there. I look back out the window and she is gone.

23

DANELLE AND I LAPSED back into our old habits. Sex, sex, and more sex. The girl is insatiable, and as ephemeral as our relationship may be, I wanted to take full advantage of the opportunity that was thrust upon me. She even agreed to go out to dinner with me one night—a first. She suggested a winery west of town, called Sander's Ridge, which was having a special dinner one Saturday night. It was about forty minutes away, out Reynolda Road, in Yadkin County, in the middle of North Carolina's wine country. We arrived a little early and sat on the wide front porch, in rocking chairs, and drank a glass of noble grape wine. Then we split another bottle over dinner, which was fantastic. Why Danelle wanted to come way out here was a mystery to me, but I'm glad we did.

The dinner, wine, and drive home seemed to dampen Danelle's enthusiasm for love-making a bit. When she dozed off after round two, I was able to sneak away and get back home about 11:00 that night. I was still thinking about my encounter with the "woman" at the coffee shop when I walked in my house and saw the message light blinking. The message was from Mary. "Jerry, I know you're disappointed, but can't we still be friends? Can you play tennis with me tomorrow...please? Let me know."

Well, Danelle and I don't usually do two nights in a row—I'm not as young as I used to be. So, I guess I'll accept Mary's invitation and hit tennis balls with her. She could always beat me in high school, and since I rarely play anymore, I may really embarrass myself playing her now. We set up a time to meet at the tennis courts at Hanes Park. Mary is there on the court bouncing a ball impatiently and waiting for me to arrive. She's wearing a tennis skirt and tank top—you've got to be kidding me. Since tennis is mostly a dying sport, there was no one else playing—just us.

We volleyed a bit and Mary ran down every errant shot I hit—not hit errantly on purpose, I'm just not very good. Finally, I couldn't take it any longer and I called her to come up to the net. Dang, she looked good! "Mary," I said, "if we continue playing tennis, or go hiking, or do anything else together...you're going to have to start wearing a bra. I'm sorry, I know you're gay, but I can't help it. I'm still a male and all your bouncing and jiggling around is like tempting a little kid with a candy bar, then not letting him eat it. I can't take it."

Mary looked at me, and at first I thought she was going to start crying. Then she smiled and said, "That's probably the nicest thing anybody's ever said to me. I understand, Jerry. Why didn't you tell me sooner?"

"Because, I enjoyed the bouncing and jiggling earlier, when I thought things might be different. But different it is. So, no more tennis tonight. Let's go get something to eat, okay?" Mary was perceptive enough to put a sweatshirt on over her tank top before we arrived at Finnegan's Wake—I love the grilled steak sandwich they have there. Mary ordered a salad with a glass of water. I got the sandwich and a Guinness. Immediately, our conversations were as comfortable as an old pair of pajamas. She told me about her girlfriend and asked me about Joel, and any other strange occurrences—I lied to her. I think she knew it was a lie, but she's a good old girl.

I didn't tell her about Joel's prediction concerning me and Ida. Why? Because it's crazy! I didn't tell her about Danelle. Why? Because I don't want her to think I'm a slut. That, and because...she's Mary. Even though I know she's gay. Even though I know I will never be with her sexually. Even though I know all these things—and I do--there's still that minor, nagging thought, stuck way back in the far quadrant of my feeble mind, that's saying, "She might change her mind. She might see how really neat and good and handsome and wonderful you are, Jerry. Don't give up...don't ever give up!"

Mary and I went to a movie together a couple of nights later, which was terrible. I mean, the movie was terrible—being with Mary was great. During the movie I had the strongest desire to take Mary's hand and hold it...but, I didn't. A couple of times I glanced over at her and I'm sure I saw her looking back at me— I'm sure of it. Mary did, however, keep her word to me and wore a bra. But for some cosmic twist of fate, the wearing of the bra now coincided with the wearing of short skirts. I mean short, short skirts.

I'm going to assume the movie, being so bad, is the reason Mary is so fidgety tonight. By fidgety, I mean she's crossing her legs every few minutes. I am fortunate the movie was not memorable, because each time Mary crossed her legs, my hormones caused my brain to take a leave of absence for several minutes. Mary, Mary, Mary...

So, now I have a somewhat regular routine during the week: seeing Danelle, who is once again happy to stay home and explore the worlds of salacious, steamy, erotic and wanton behaviors, and spending time with good, old-fashioned, sisterly Mary—while silently fighting off the demons inside me, who are clawing at my guts to get out.

On one of my nights off from both women, I visit my cousin Joe at the bar in H & H. Since it's a weeknight, it's not too busy and he can talk with me. I really don't go into specifics, but I do tell him I'm spending time with Mary and Danelle. He's a good listener. He obviously paid attention in Bartending School when they taught the lesson on listening. After I tell him as much as I'm willing to tell him, he nods a little more, then says, "So what you're saying is that you're seeing two women—for different reasons—but not really 'dating' either one of them. Is that the gist of it?"

Well, I guess he's right. I'm not dating Danelle, in the sense of what most people would define dating. And, I'm certainly not dating Mary—we're just friends (unfortunately). My lack of response prompts Joe to ask further, "So, you really don't see any long term romantic future with either one of them, right? I mean, you can't see yourself marrying Danelle can you?"

Quite honestly, I reply, "No, that's definitely not going to happen."

"And, as much as you're clearly smitten with the gay girl, she's obviously out of the picture romantically. So, what is your long-term plan here, numnuts?"

It's quite apparent to me now that Joe flunked the part of Bartending School where he's supposed to empathize with his customers, not call them names.

I have no long-term goal. I barely have a short-term goal. Some nights I'm thrilled to have found my way back home. The sex with Danelle is obviously nice, but...that's all there is—sex. We don't go out, we really don't talk about anything. We don't have any common interests—except satisfying each other's lustful desires. Other than that, it's really pretty boring being with Danelle. Whereas, with Mary, I LOVE being with her. Everything is fun, we enjoy the same things, our conversations are exciting and interesting, and the sex is...only in my mind.

I tried Panera once more, but the same Hispanic Assistant Manager stopped me at the door again. This time I don't even see Ida anywhere. Not that I want to. Not that I believe anything that hobo, dancing, singing, three-piece suit wearing, pseudo-angel

Joel told me. Which I don't. Roberto Barrios shot JFK? Certainly, an angel could come up with a better story than that!

All this leads me up to where I am right now, at work, caught up on everything, with time on my hands, and looking at a dating site. I'm thinking to myself, "How pathetic can you be?" Until I actually click on the site and see dozens and dozens of pictures of beautiful women. Really? Yep, Jerry old boy, you should've checked this out years ago. I fill out my information (fudged only a little, but they expect that, don't they?) then I fill out the form of what I'm looking for in a woman.

Someone within two or three of years of my age would be nice. Medium build, or slim; not too tall, not too short. College degree would be nice, but not necessary. They must have a job (I won't divulge my financial situation just yet). I really want to meet someone childless; I know this may sound harsh, but I don't think I'm equipped at the present moment to become an instant father. Hair color—I don't care. Religion—yes. Interests—I don't care.

Okay, that being done, I sincerely doubt they'll come up with a 100% match for me. Now, I have to decide how much I'm willing to settle for. If she's pretty, then I'll settle for a lot less—I think. I'm not sure. Anyway, I send off my information and pay my fee and hope I'll hear back from them by the end of the week.

Lo and behold, ninety minutes later I received an email from the dating site with the profiles of thirty-seven women who met ALL of my requirements! Wow!! I start browsing through them and eliminate several just because their appearance doesn't fulfill my expectation, a few because I know they're too pretty for me. I eliminate a few others because they don't live in Winston-Salem, and one is eliminated because she looks too much like Mary. I'm left now with fourteen women who seem to be very attractive and who possess all the pre-requisites I listed. I send off these fourteen choices back to the dating site and they will somehow match these women and see if I have met any of their expectations—therefore, finding a MATCH!

This match-making process took a little longer than I expected. I didn't hear back from them for two complete days. They now have four women that I chose, who chose me back. That's a little disappointing to me. It means that of the fourteen women I chose, ten of them did not choose me back. My feelings are a little hurt; however, the four that chose me back are beauties indeed. Now, the hard part: I have to meet them. This is a pretty good week for setting up "blind dates" with these women because Danelle is in Richmond, Virginia for training all week and I can always find time on short notice to do something with Mary.

The first woman I called, Wendy, never answered the phone. I called her several times during the day and night and she never answered for two consecutive days. I'll put her on the back burner. The second woman, Elizabeth, told me she just met someone yesterday that she really likes, but she'll call me if it doesn't work out with this guy. Okay. I set up "dates" or, I'm not sure what it's actually called, meetings maybe, with the last two—Lynn and Sara.

Lynn was very nice and attractive, but I don't think I overly impressed her. She was a legal analyst, whatever that is, and I'm pretty sure my position at the waste management company didn't fulfill her expectations. It was pleasant, but . . .

I had a fun "date" with Sara. She was easy to talk with and nice to look at. We had several things in common and even went to UNC-G at the same time, but didn't know each other there. We met over drinks and I truly thought Sara would be someone I'd like to continue seeing—until we got ready to leave and she asked me, "Jerry, would you like to come over to my house and meet my mom? She's great and I know she'd enjoy seeing you."

"Oh, wow...I'd really like to Sara," NOT, "but I've got to get home and finish up some reports for work in the morning."

"Oh, I'm sorry, Jerry. Maybe you could come to dinner with me and my mom this weekend?"

"Yeah, let me look at my calendar, Sara. I'll give you a call when I see how things are scheduled."

"Great! I can't wait for you to meet my mom. She's the greatest!"

Well, Jerry, old boy...maybe the dating site experience was not the best idea in the world. I can still try to call the first woman on my list, Wendy, who never answered her phone. Nah, let it go. I've still got Danelle and Mary. And...I'm a pathetic loser.

24

MARY INVITED ME to her house for dinner Saturday night with some friends she said I might like. I hope Mary isn't trying to set me up with someone. I sort of dreaded going over and thought seriously about making up an excuse to get out of it. It turned out the "friends" were the preacher, Will, and his wife, Liz. We did have a good time sitting around talking before dinner. Will's wife had a good sense of humor. Since everyone else is always coming to her husband for advice, I asked her if she also asked him for advice with anything. She said, "Of course I do. With kids around the house, I needed to find some peace, so I asked Will how I could achieve true inner peace. He told me the key is to always finish what I start. So far, I've finished two bags of M & M's and a chocolate cake. I feel better already."

After dinner, the fun stopped when the real reason we were all there came out: Will's wife wanted to hear my story of Joel and the other occurrences I've had. When this subject came up, I looked at Will, because I specifically remember asking him if our conversations were in strict confidence. He knew why I looked at him and said, "Not me! Mary and Liz. I've not said a word and told them not to involve me at all."

I looked at Mary and she said, "What? I didn't know it was a secret."

Before I knew what to say, Liz jumped in and said, "Don't be mad at her, Jerry. She mentioned it to me one night and I bugged her and bugged her to tell me more. She finally told me a little, just to shut me up. Will never would say a word—even when I threatened him! See, in school, before we were married, I wrote my thesis on supernatural beings, messengers, and angelic apparitions. Even though I did a ton of study and reading and research, I never—not once—ever met anyone who might have actually had a true experience." We were all quiet for a moment, then she continued: "Obviously, you don't have to say anything, but I am truly fascinated and would love to hear about it."

I looked at her and said, "Liz, you won't believe anything I tell you—just like them."

She never took her eyes off me and replied, "Jerry, in the dark of the night, every atheist half believes."

I wanted to tell her my story. I wanted someone to tell me the whole, entire, wild, bizarre saga was a bunch of bull crap. But deep down, I was half afraid someone would tell me it was all true—and that was what I was not sure I can handle. So, I leaned back in my chair, glancing at Mary's legs, in her short skirt, and said, "Liz, sometimes a cigar...is just a cigar."

No one said anything, so I got up and walked to the door to leave. Mary followed me over and said that she was sorry she'd told Liz anything of our private conversations. I believed her; I wasn't mad about that. Heck, I wasn't mad at all. I just wanted to think, I wanted to believe. I wanted to convince myself that sometimes a hobo...is just a hobo."

After a couple of weeks, I tried going back to my original Panera. Maybe my ban had been lifted. Nope. They stopped me when I walked in. I tried to ask them how long my banishment lasted, but they wouldn't even talk to me. On the way back to work I stopped at a Starbucks. When I walked in, I remembered all the reasons I don't go to Starbucks. So, I stopped at McDonald's and got a coffee and a plain biscuit—my life is really going downhill.

At least I'll be able to see Danelle tonight and forget all my troubles for a few hours.

Danelle is unusually quiet, even for her. Our "date" usually lasts three to four hours, but, tonight, after her initial desires were met, she rolls over in bed and says, "Jerry, I've got something to tell you." Well, this should be very interesting—she never tells me anything, except which position to move into. She props herself up on her elbow and looks at me, then says, "I'm getting married. This might be the last time we see each other, but I'll let you know."

I initially thought she wanted to marry me. No. Fortunately, that is not what she was saying. I answered, "You're getting married? Did I hear that correctly?"

"Yes, I've been putting it off, but I can't keep postponing it any longer. He's getting suspicious."

It was difficult for me to process this, it sounded so bizarre. I asked, "Who is it that you're marrying?"

She rolls over on top of me and says, "You met him at that taco restaurant that night...remember?"

I did remember seeing her the night I cancelled our date and was with Mary. Danelle was with the same older man I'd seen at her condo that day. But I certainly didn't "meet" him. Just to confirm, I asked, "Do you mean the older guy?"

Danelle doesn't initially answer because she was in the process of trying to engage us in a coital moment. "Danelle, stop! How can you tell me you're getting married and still do what you're trying to do?"

She seems offended, and says, "This is just sex, Jerry. It's not serious."

"But getting married is serious, Danelle! Don't you love this guy?"

"Well, yeah...sort of."

I half push her off me and say, "Sort of? What does that mean? I can't believe you're still seeing me while you're planning on marrying this other guy."

She becomes a little offended and replies, "Well, Jerry, one has nothing to do with the other. After I'm married, I doubt we'll be able to see each other very often anyway."

I am not nearly millennial enough to understand or comprehend what is happening here. I simply say, "I'm leaving, Danelle. Good luck with everything." Even after me saying this, even after this entire weird conversation, she still tries to put her hands in my pants as I'm getting dressed. I eventually make it out the door and into my car, but I have to admit, my head is spinning a little.

The next day I receive two phone calls from Danelle, but let them both go to voice mail. The first message says she's sorry, but hopes we can still be "friends." The second message asks what I'm doing tonight. Ever since I inherited all the money, my life has gone downhill. I start falling for a girl who's gay. I meet a woman who takes me places I never knew existed sexually, and she gets married—sort of. I get banned from Panera. Then get banned from the other Panera. All the while, striking out with the dating site. I'm feeling so sorry for myself that even the bad-old days with Jennifer are starting to seem pretty good to me now.

I need help. Panera can't ban me forever, so I call their toll-free number and speak with a very nice lady. I tell her my entire, strange saga (most of it anyway) and she seems very sympathetic. She tells me someone will contact me soon. She was right. I'd given her my email address and within the hour I received a notice from Panera that my banishment had ended, but I was on probation. If I didn't cause any trouble for ninety days, my record would be wiped clean. I'm back in business!

Immediately upon getting the news, I head over there—excited and hungry. There are several new people working here now and a new manager and assistant manager since Ida transferred. Only a couple of people in line; it's a good day. "What can I get for you, sir?"

I'm so excited I can hardly get the words out: "Blueberry bagel, extra toasted, with peanut butter, and a small coffee, please. Thanks."

"We don't have any peanut butter. Is cream cheese okay?"

No, no, no, no, no! Not again. No, please, no. "You used to have peanut butter here, do you mind checking?"

"Sure, hold on." She takes two steps towards the kitchen and yells to no one in particular that I can see, saying, "Do we have peanut butter?" I don't hear anyone answer or see anyone acknowledge her question, but she turns back to me and says, "No, sir. We don't have any."

Jerry...don't blow it! Don't lose your temper. Don't be a jerk! Just smile and say okay. "Okay. Coffee and a cinnamon/raisin bagel. Thank you." As a mild form of protest, when I get the bagel, with cream cheese, I walk to the nearest trash can and dump the cream cheese in it. I'm sure they don't care, one way or the other, but it made me feel good. I put a lid on the coffee and take my bagel back to my car, stopping momentarily, looking for any homeless men that may be near. I didn't see any, so I started the drive over to the other Panera near Hanes Mall.

As I walked in the store, the Hispanic Assistant Manager confronts me again. Before anything is said, Ida comes around the counter and says, "It's okay, Pedro, he can come in again." She doesn't even look at me or say anything to me. She simply turns around and walks back into the kitchen out of view. It was indeed worth the trip. They have peanut butter and plenty of bagels and hot coffee. Everything is copacetic—except for Ida ignoring me, the long drive over here, and the nasty looks Pedro keeps giving me. But, as they say, when I've got peanut butter in my mouth, I don't care what anyone thinks.

This has all taken so long, I call work and tell them I am going to take the rest of the day off as vacation. I've been thinking about buying a new car since I have the money now. I've never actually had a new, new car; I've always bought used cars in the past. As I'm daydreaming about cars, walking towards mine, I'm stopped in my tracks. Joel is standing next to my car--back in his hobo clothing. He says, "I like this car, Jerry. What's wrong with it?"

"So, you're a hobo again?"

"No, Jerry. I'm just a friend coming to say hello and goodbye again."

"Joel, you aren't my friend. I don't know what you are, or who you are, but you're not my friend."

"Jerry, I just want to help you do the right thing. That's all."

I look at Joel several seconds before answering, then reply, "I don't need any help doing the right thing. In fact, I don't believe anything you've ever told me. Ida?? That's the craziest piece of garbage you've ever said. All of that stuff about me having a daughter and my granddaughter saving some guy's life...what a bunch of crap! I don't know what your story is Joel, or what the point of all this craziness is, but I'm sick of it. I don't believe you and I don't want to see you again. Is that clear?"

The grin came off his face and he looks seriously at me and replies, "I'm sorry you feel that way, Jerry. I'll leave for now, not because you requested it, but because I have other business to attend to. However, just so you'll know that everything I've told you is the truth, you're going to see three signs that will convince you of that fact."

"What do you mean, three signs?"

"You'll know. There's my bus. Goodbye, Jerry."

Joel walks away and I get in my car trying to convince myself that he's only a weird hobo, trying to mess with my mind. But, why is he messing with my mind? I don't believe any of this. I don't believe in any signs and I don't believe in smiling, singing hobos!

25

I'VE ALWAYS LIKED the way Saabs look. I decided my first car shopping visit would be to the local Saab dealership to see what sort of deal they could offer. I was a little surprised to find, through my searches online, that a new BMW (not one of the big ones) or Mercedes or Saab or Lexus was really not that much more expensive than a new Jeep or Chrysler or Toyota or Honda. Even though I could afford anything I wanted, that didn't mean I was going to go crazy. I still wanted a good deal.

I drove into the Saab dealership on Silas Creek Parkway and a very attractive young lady came out to help. She offered fresh coffee as well. We walked around and she told me about all the various styles--much, much more than I really wanted to know. I found one model that I really liked: It was deep blue with more features than I ever realized came with a car. It was $37,190 as is, or a few features could be added for a little extra. I took it out for a short test drive and it was indeed a dream. I wanted it. When I came back from the test drive, we stood there discussing it and the sales lady kept telling me all the various advantages and extras I could get.

Then I noticed a banner that was hanging over the showroom about a contest they were having. I asked Kali, the saleslady, what it was about and she showed me on her ipad she was carrying. Today was the last day of the event, which gave anyone who signed the papers to buy a car a chance to spin a wheel and get a discount on the car. The wheel was inside the showroom and the amounts shown ranged from $100 all the way up to $20,000. It looked as though there were about fifty numbers on the wheel. Most of the discounts were in the $250-$1,000 range. One was for $5,000 and then the big one for $20,000. I presumed that somehow the wheel was rigged to never fall on the $20,000 number.

After a little haggling, where they always "pretend" to give you a break, I decided to buy this car. I didn't want to shop any further. I liked the idea of having a car most people didn't. There are a lot of BMWs out there and Mercedes and Lexuses...but not a lot of Saabs. Especially a pretty one like this. We went to Kali's desk and signed papers and drank coffee and shook hands with the sales manager and others, whose jobs I didn't know. Then, they all took me out to the wheel to give it a spin and made a big deal out of it. All the sales people came in to look and I went over and Kali said, "Good luck, Mr. McRacken. Give it a whirl." And I did.

It went round and round and started slowing, slowing, slowing, and finally stopped on a $250 discount slot--except, it didn't stop. When we all thought it had stopped and the sales manager started to say "Congratulations" even before he got the word out, the wheel clicked one more time and landed on the $20,000 slot— and stayed there!

There was absolute pandemonium in the showroom. The sales manager was gesturing to all the other people who worked there, and Kali stood stunned, with her mouth open. Several other customers who witnessed everything came to shake my hand and take pictures of the wheel with their cell phones. It was a wild few moments. The Sales Manager and his staff went into a nearby office and I could see arms waving and fingers pointing and I could tell something was happening that was not good—for them. But, the bottom line was that I just bought a $37,190 car for $17,190. I was happy, even though they clearly were not.

They were going to clean up the car and told me I could come back in a couple of hours to pick it up. No one but Kali shook my hand as I walked away. I got on Silas Creek Parkway and started driving, happy with my purchase and stunned at my good fortune. I thought to myself: "I'd have never been that lucky if I really needed that money." And then it hit me...Joel had said, THREE SIGNS. Was this one of the three signs? No, it couldn't be. No way, this was just good fortune. I was simply lucky—that's all there is to it. Pure and simple luck. Sounded good—but I couldn't convince myself that it was just indeed pure and simple luck.

I came back in a couple of hours to pick up my new car, but didn't see Kali, the Sales Manager, or any other sales people. A guy from the garage came out and handed me the keys and said, "If I were you, I'd go to Vegas. No one has ever spun that wheel and gotten anything over $250. You are one lucky son-of-a-gun. Good luck, sir!"

But I knew luck had nothing to do with it. I left a message on Mary's phone and asked if she wanted to get together tonight. She called me back, but I had my phone hooked up to the hands free phone system in the car, and couldn't figure out how to use it. She hung up and I called her back immediately. I was excited about my car and wanted to show it to Mary. She answered the phone with hello and then broke into tears. I said, "Mary, what's wrong?"

She couldn't answer because of the sobs and tears. Finally, she said, "Teri just broke up with me." Teri was her girlfriend, stationed in Afghanistan with the Army. "She called me and told me she's met someone over there and they're in love."

"I'm so sorry, Mary. I don't know what to say."

"I should've seen it coming, Jerry. Her letters have gone from nearly every day, to once a week, now every two or three weeks. And, she never answers my calls or Skypes me back. I knew something was wrong, but I was hoping she was just busy. I don't know what to do, Jerry."

"Do you want me to come over tonight and we can talk about it?"

"Thanks, Jerry, but I think I just want to be alone. I'll call you tomorrow."

We hung up, but hearing this news, that broke my friend's heart, has taken all the luster off my new car happiness.

With Mary home suffering and no more Danelle, for the time being, I'm left to going downtown to see my cousin Joe. I have to tell someone about my new car; the excitement is killing me. Parking is always a burden down here because the restaurants and pubs and activity of the downtown area have outgrown the available parking spaces. Just as I passed his bar, I see a space open and I quickly stop to parallel park, hoping I don't hit something in the tight space. There's a large beverage truck in front of me that takes up too much room, but I'll be okay if I'm careful.

Everything's fine, a little tight, but I'm okay. I check the cell phone and take a deep whiff of that new car smell before getting out--sweet! I get out, hit the automatic lock, and BOOM!! The lift gate on the rear end of the beverage truck suddenly had collapsed down on to my car, smashing the hood and roof, right where I'd been sitting not twenty seconds ago. It happened so fast and so violently that it almost didn't seem real. But it was. My beautiful new car was smashed to pieces by the lift gate and ramp from this truck. Twenty seconds earlier and I would have been smashed as well...twenty seconds.

The police came, a tow-truck took my new, worthless car away, and I was left shaken, stunned, and thinking, "The SECOND SIGN."

I went back to the Saab dealership the next day only to find that Kali didn't work there any longer. No one would say why. They didn't have another car like the one I bought, but I did pick one out that was close. It would be okay. It cost me some extra insurance money. I'd only driven my new car less than fifty miles, but somehow the value of it had shrunk by nearly $8,000. Go figure that out!

I spent the next day telling and re-telling my story to everyone at work. Mary still didn't feel like doing anything—I understand. I went to Panera (the one where Ida worked) for my morning sabbatical; if Ida's there and wants to hear my story, I might tell her. Or, maybe I won't. She wasn't there. At least she never appears while I'm there. But it's okay; peanut butter, bagel, and coffee have a way of making everything alright.

It's nice to sit and sip and reflect. I don't see anyone I know or recognize at this new Panera. There seems to be a different crowd here than at the old one. Maybe because it's near the mall, I'm not sure, but the people are different. I have time to contemplate and ruminate over the past few days and truly think about what has happened. Certainly, winning the $20,000 on the wheel was unusual. And narrowly avoiding being smashed by the ramp and lift gate was very fortunate—but are these truly SIGNS? Am I reading too much into this? I might be giving Joel too much credit. This is all just coincidence. Right?

The next day, Mary calls me at work and asks if I want to come over to her house tonight. She says she'll cook us a pizza: goat cheese, artichokes, and mushrooms...Lordy, the things I'll do for my friend. I smell the pizza cooking when I come in Mary's house. I also notice Mary has on a man's button up shirt, with a few buttons unbuttoned—and she's NOT wearing a bra. Oh, devil inside me, please be easy; you know I can resist everything except temptation.

Mary gave me a Michelob Ultra and she had water...well, if the truth be known, we both had water. We had a small salad with our pizza. Mary seemed to enjoy hers; I did not enjoy mine, but I did enjoy the view. We sat on the couch after eating and Mary told me all about Teri and their relationship. She had a second bottle of water and she even gave me a second Mich Ultra. I'm assuming she thought I'd get waterlogged before I got drunk.

She cried a little, not much. She just needed to tell someone what happened, and I was glad that someone was me. As she was talking, she would lean forward to reach her water bottle on the table, and I'm almost certain that I saw some things I probably shouldn't have seen between those loose buttons on her shirt. Then, to my surprise, Mary said, "Do you want to play Scrabble?"

"Scrabble? You mean the game?" I was totally bumfuzzled by this question.

"Yes," she said. "It'll be fun, and it'll take my mind off things."

Mary set the board up, while I tried my level-headed best not to look down her shirt. She then got out the little pieces with the alphabet letters on them. She dropped a few, then took a handful and tossed them over to me. She must've thrown about eight or ten pieces over my way. All but three of them were face down so I couldn't see what letters they were. Three pieces were face up. Three pieces lined up and were facing me. Three pieces spelled a name. Those three letters Mary picked up randomly and threw my way were: I D A.

Mary explained the rules to me as I sat there staring at those letters: I D A.

She said, "Jerry, are you listening to me?"

"Yeah, I'm good." In reality, I had no clue. I did not understand what just happened. My mind is racing at warp speed, and I'm sure somewhere, over the rainbow, Joel is sitting around with a great big smile on his face.

We played Scrabble and I let Mary win every game to take her mind off her trouble—I'm good that way. We didn't discuss Teri anymore; we didn't really discuss anything that I can remember. Finally, Mary folded up the board game and gathered up all the pieces. She took the empty bottles back to her recycling bin and walked me to the door. She said, "Thanks for everything, Jerry. I don't know what I'd do if I lost you." Then she gave me a long, tight hug that truly did not feel like a "friend" hug. But, maybe I'm hallucinating--it has been a weird night.

26

MARY AND I HAVE BEEN DOING something together nearly every night now. We love talking and simply enjoying each other's company, and it seems so natural being with her. Our only disagreement was that she wanted me to buy a Prius instead of the Saab. Mary...you'll have to unbutton a LOT more buttons for me to be buying a Prius.

She received a letter one day from Teri, her ex-girlfriend. She didn't want to open it. She asked me if I'd read it and let her know if there was anything worthwhile in it. She was trying to put the pain and heartache behind her and didn't want to be reminded of anything. It seemed a little awkward, but I agreed to read it later.

We went to the Par Course on Silas Creek Parkway and walked around the track until dark. Afterwards Mary wanted to go home and wash clothes—in reality, she wanted me to go home and read the letter, then let her know if there was anything in it that might hint of a reconciliation with her and Teri. I dropped her off at her house and she opened the door and said, "Call me later?"

I was questioning myself about the letter. Would I tell Mary the truth if it indeed hinted at reconciliation? Of course I would...I hope. I made myself an Iron Maiden and sat down to read it. It was not an appeal for reconciliation. In fact, it was a letter of accusation. In a general, roundabout way, Teri was accusing Mary of forcing her to find another "love" because Mary was having second thoughts about a man! About a man??

So, Teri, in her selfish, egotistical way, was accusing Mary of causing their breakup, because she "thought" Mary was interested in a man. Thank you, Teri! Is this true? Or is this only an excuse Teri is using because she dumped Mary. And, if it is true...then WHO is this man? Is it me? Is Mary interested in me? I need another Iron Maiden—or two.

I called Mary and told her the letter was a feeble attempt by Teri to apologize for the breakup, and in no way hinted at a reconciliation. Mary said, "Burn it. I don't want it back in my house." Should I mention the thing about "a man"? No, Jerry, let it go for now. There's plenty of time.

Each day this week I made the drive to the Panera near Hanes Mall, through all that nasty traffic, just to have my peanut butter. There might be something wrong with me. I have a nice toasted bagel and fresh, hot coffee each morning. And I didn't see Ida all week. I thought she might be working different hours, but when I asked the cashier about her, she said Ida was indeed there and was usually out front with them all the time. Hmm.

The most fun nights spent with Mary are the times we do nothing. Just sitting around talking, or watching television are the best times. She has totally reverted to her braless days. I don't mind and I don't bring it up—but she has to know. At any rate, we're having fun. Each night, when I leave, we hug tightly and long. If feels good. I've made up my mind that I will not broach the subject of a "relationship" with Mary. I will not try to kiss her again—unless she kisses me first. And, I will be whatever she wants me to be. I'm happy with that...for now.

Saturday morning I get a phone call from a number I don't recognize. I answer and say "Hello," but there's only silence on the other end. I almost hang up when I hear a woman's voice. She says, "Is this Jerry, from the dating site?"

The dating site? I'd completely forgotten about that misadventure. I have no idea what this is about, but I answer, "Yes, this is Jerry. Who is this?"

"My name's Elizabeth. You called me one night, but I'd just met someone else. I told you I'd let you know if things didn't work out. So, I'm calling."

I think I remember that now. "So, things didn't work out well, I guess."

She says, "Well, it was okay, but I don't think I was what he was looking for. Probably not pretty enough." I thought this was very odd that a woman would ever say, or admit, that she didn't think she was pretty enough. It intrigued me. I had deleted all the dating site information I had, and I really didn't remember anything about this woman Elizabeth. I guess I was silent a little too long as I thought about this, because she then says, "Sorry if I bothered you. I just thought you might want to meet. But it's okay if you don't—I understand."

I'm in a dilemma. I'm having a great time with Mary. I want to be with Mary. But I'm still unsure about things with her. And now, this phone call. There's something about Elizabeth's voice that is comforting and familiar—the kind of voice that makes you want to keep talking with her. I guess I'm taking too long thinking again because she says, "Are you still there?"

"Yes, I'm sorry. Your call surprised me a little." Quick boy, think! I have plans with Mary tonight and tomorrow night. "Would you like to meet for a drink or something tomorrow afternoon? That's pretty safe for us, don't you think?"

After a moment or two of silence she answers, "Sure, how about TJ's Deli on Country Club Road about 3:00?"

I think that was a fairly weird choice for us to meet, but I say, "Great. I'll see you then. Thanks for calling, Elizabeth."

Mary and I are going to a movie tonight at the Aperture Theater downtown. It's something artsy I think, I'm not sure. As long as they have popcorn and Mary's there, I'll be fine. Then my phone rings again and it's Mary. I hope she's not cancelling our date for tonight? Is it a date? Shut up and answer the phone! "Hey, what's up, Mary?"

"Hey, Jerry. Everything okay?"

This seems a bit strange. Why is she asking me if everything is okay? Is she cancelling our "date" for tonight?

"Yeah, everything's good. Are we still on for tonight?" I need to find out now.

"Of course we are—I'm looking forward to it. I'm calling because I have a favor to ask."

"Sure, anything. You know that. What do you need?"

I heard Mary take a deep breath before she answered, then she began, "Jerry, please don't be mad at me, and I understand if you say no, but . . ."

"What? Mary, just tell me. It's okay."

"Is there any way possible you can spend a few minutes with Liz, the preacher's wife, this afternoon and tell her a little about your 'encounters?' You don't have to tell her everything. Just maybe what you told me, or less. Whatever you're comfortable with. She's driving me crazy every time I see her now. She's just obsessed with hearing about your so-called angel meetings."

If it had been anyone else in the entire world asking me that question, I'd flat out say NO. However, Mary knew, and I knew, that I cannot say no to her.

"Jerry, are you still there? You're not mad at me are you?"

"No...it's okay. What time? And I don't want to go to her house."

Mary says, "Okay, I'll tell her to come to my house and I'll take a walk around the block and leave you two alone. Thanks, Jerry. I'll make it up to you—I promise."

If Mary's going to "make it up to me" I'll not only talk to Liz but with Beelzebub, Lucifer, Richard Nixon, Linda Blair, or any other demons available.

When I arrive at Mary's house, Liz is already there. Mary hands me a bottle of water and excuses herself to take a walk. We both sit but not together. She's on the couch with a notebook. I take a chair across from her. I've already decided that I'll not volunteer anything. I'll only answer direct questions and nothing more-- maybe not even that!

Liz starts, "Mary has only told me that you think you met an angel, nothing more than that. I tried to get her to elaborate but that's all she's told me. So, I guess the big, overriding question I have is just that...did you, in fact, meet an angel?"

Alright, how do I answer this? Do I even know if Joel, or any of the others, were in fact true angels? No, I don't know for sure; however, they were something. There has been something going on—I just don't know what.

"Jerry, are you okay?"

"Yeah, I was only considering how to answer your question. And, the answer is 'yes' I think I have. With the emphasis being on the word 'think.' Does that make sense?"

"Why are you unsure if you did?"

"Because the main person, or angel, or whatever he is, also met your husband and met Mary, and neither one of them thinks he was an angel. That's why. Plus, he's told me things that I think are just ridiculous, which I'm not going into, by the way."

She takes a few moments for this to register. I don't think she knew her husband had met Joel. Then, she said, "But why did YOU think he was an angel?" Before I could answer, she asks another question, "Did he look like an angel?"

The opening I was looking for..."What does an angel look like, Liz?"

But, she didn't answer that, instead, she asks, "If he was, or is, an angel, why do you think he picked you to come and visit?"

"He had something to tell me. He had a plan he wanted to make sure I followed. He wanted me to be on the right path to ensure this plan would indeed happen."

She thinks about this, writes something in her notebook, then asks, "Was he trying to force you to do something against your will?"

"No, nothing like that. In fact, he kept insisting that I have the free will to do anything I want to do. But he wanted me to know the ramifications and implications of each decision I would make. Does that make sense?"

I can tell that it makes no sense to her. She is looking at me with a blank expression on her face, wondering what in the world do I ask now. Finally, she continues, "Have you met more than one angel?"

"I've had encounters with several beings, human or otherwise, that were unworldly and strange. Encounters that I have no explanation for."

She was writing furiously in her notebook now, and asks, "Can you tell me about any of these encounters?"

I did not want to elaborate, or get into discussions about this, but think I'll give her a few instances just to peak her curiosity. "I met a saleslady in a jewelry store who disappeared. I saw a farmer, who no one else happened to see, who saved my life. I saw quarters disappear from a man's hand—then he disappeared. And, I was told I'd be given three signs—and I was indeed given three signs. There are more, but that's all I'm going to say."

Liz has stopped her scribbling but has not closed her open mouth. We sit for a moment staring at each other. Finally, after she closes her mouth, I say, "Liz, I think that's enough. I need to be going."

She puts her hand up and pleads, "Can I just ask you one more question, Jerry? Please?"

"Okay, go ahead."

"What do you think they were all trying to tell you?"

"Liz, I don't 'think' – I know what they were telling me."

Now, I wanted to make her wait a few seconds before I continued. She can't stand it and excitedly asks, "What??"

"They all wanted me to know who the woman is that I will marry."

This leaves Liz speechless, if that's possible. I get up, and when I did, Mary walked in the door. I think she must've been outside waiting—I'm not sure. I look at Mary and say, "See you later tonight, okay?" Then I look back at Liz and say, "See you later Liz, I hope that helped." She only sits there staring back at me, not moving, not responding.

27

THE MOVIE AT THE APERTURE Theater was indeed artsy. None of it made sense to me, but it did make Mary cry a little, so I guess it was good—or not, I have no clue. The popcorn was good; I ate all mine and most of Mary's. And, she gave me an extra-long hug when I left her house later. I thought it might turn into a kiss, but it didn't. That's okay; the hug was good. Mary invited me to go to church with her Sunday morning and I probably would've gone if it hadn't been for the conversation with Liz yesterday. I just didn't want to "accidentally" run into her again.

I decide to drive over to Panera, just to have something to do until my "meeting," or "date," or whatever it's called this afternoon, with Elizabeth, the woman from the dating service. Again, I don't see Ida. I don't really know if she works weekends or weekdays or what. Since the run-in I had that day with her, I never see her anymore. After I'm filled, I decide to ride around town a little in my new car. I really liking it; it drives like a dream. I decide to take a college tour around town. I first drive over to Salem College and cruise through the quaint little streets in and around the college and Old Salem, where almost everyone I see is old. I wonder if that's just a coincidence.

Then, I drive over to the North Carolina School of the Arts and make my way around campus there. I pull in a parking area and turn the car off because I see a group of students walking my way and I wanted to look at them. Not in a weird way, but in an interested, never-seen-that before way. Then, after my curiosity was satiated, I rode through Winston-Salem State University and marveled at the new buildings and impressiveness of the school.

It had been years since I'd been on campus and I was amazed at all the changes. Finally, I make it over to Wake Forest and drive through the campus, looking at all the license plates on the student cars that aren't from North Carolina. That, too, is amazing, and I get few second looks from the Wake students at my new Saab. I love my car.

Time to get home, take a shower, and meet Elizabeth today at TJ's Deli. I'm still perplexed by her choice of meeting places. I start watching a TV show on the death of Dennis Wilson, one of the Beach Boys, and lose track of time. Then, as it always is when you're running late, I catch every red light available. I pull into the parking lot about 3:03 and walk into TJ's Deli for the first time in my life. For security reasons, all the dating website provides is a person's first name and a small profile with a picture of that person. Remembering her picture, I knew Elizabeth was attractive, with medium brown hair, which looked like it might be permed—I wasn't sure. It was a small picture, so it was difficult to tell much of anything else.

I see about fifteen tables spread around the deli, most of them empty. Two tables have couples sitting there and one table has an older man drinking a beer—I didn't know they served beer here. And the only other table has a woman sitting by herself. When she sees me, she waves a little feminine wave, like women do. First impressions: she is definitely pretty, nice smile, nice hair (I think it is permed a bit), she seems in good shape, but it's hard to tell how tall she is since she's still sitting down.

I quickly walk over and pull out a chair across from her at the small table, and say, "Hi, Elizabeth. Nice to meet you."

She smiles back and replies, "It's nice to see you again too, Jerry."

I think I may have misunderstood her. Did she just say, "It's nice to see you AGAIN . . ."? Or was my mind playing tricks on me? I try not to stare too hard, but I need to make sure I don't know this woman--I don't. Oh, no! I hope this isn't one of Joel's friends. So, I ask her, "Have we met before?"

"Yes, Jerry. We've met a lot of times before."

Oh, my God! Another angel meeting. Just what I need! I do not want to play this game with her, so I just point blank ask her, "Alright, just tell me up front, are you an angel or not?"

She looks at me rather oddly and says, "An angel?"

"Yes, are you an angel?"

The smile disappears from her face and she looks at me and says, "No, Jerry. I'm Ida."

The next thing I remember, the older man, who was drinking the beer across the room, is wiping my face with a wet napkin. I look at his bushy eyebrows and say, "What are you doing?"

"Are you okay? I think you passed out. Do you need to lie down?"

"No, I don't need to lie down. What are you talking about?"

Then Ida, or Elizabeth (I'm confused) speaks, and says, "Jerry, you slumped over and your eyes closed. What happened?"

The older guy starts wiping my forehead again and I have to brush his hand away.

"I'm fine...I'm fine. Everything's okay."

The older man ambles back to his seat muttering something. This woman sitting in front of me, takes my hand and asks, "Are you really okay? Do you need to go to the emergency room?"

Am I in a bad dream? What in the San Juan Hill is happening here? I look over at her and say, "I'm fine. Who are you?"

"I'm Ida, Jerry."

I'm totally confused. "Ida who?"

"Jerry...Ida from Panera."

I think my eyeballs are going to explode. I look back at her and she says again, "Ida. From Panera."

"I was supposed to meet a woman named Elizabeth. And, you're not the Ida I know from Panera."

She smiles and says, "Yes, I am."

Finding this hard to believe, I ask, "Are you sure?"

"Well, I think I know who I am! I'm Ida, Jerry. I'm not an angel and I work at Panera.

This can't be. The Ida I know always wears a floppy Panera uniform and wears a Panera hat. The Ida I know always has her hair tied in a ponytail behind the hat. The Ida I know never wears makeup. The Ida I know isn't anywhere near this pretty! Of course, I don't say any of this out loud.

We sit for a few moments looking at each other and I just now realize she's still holding my hand. It feels good, so I don't move it. Finally, I say, "I was supposed to meet someone named Elizabeth."

"I know. That's my middle name. I used it on the dating site just to be careful in case I met a weirdo."

"I didn't recognize you. You don't look the same."

She laughs a little and says, "Well I don't wear my uniform everywhere I go, Jerry."

We continue sitting and staring at each other, still holding hands. Finally she speaks again, "The day you first called, it surprised me. I knew it was you; I recognized your picture. I was pretty sure you didn't recognize me. I didn't really have a date that night, I was just afraid—or unsure if I really wanted to meet you socially. It is a bit odd between us, isn't it?"

Not really knowing how to respond to that, I say, "It is something, Ida. I'm not sure how to describe it."

When I said that, she slowly slides her hand away from mine. Then she says, "Well, I guess it was a mistake for us to meet like this."

"No, it's not a mistake, Ida. I'm just surprised. I'm...I'm surprised."

She looks at me and nods a little, saying, "Look, Jerry, I'm going to leave now. You have my number. If you ever want to get together under 'normal' circumstances, just give me a call. I'm sorry to have misled you." Then Ida rises from the table to leave and I only then realize she has on a fairly short skirt that revealed a spectacular pair of legs. She opens the door and, looking back at me, asks, "Are you going to be alright, Jerry?"

I nod and she continues out the door, but I am absolutely, totally unsure if I am ever going to be alright. Ida...I had no idea! She's pretty and nice and has great legs. How could I have missed this before? What do I do now?

28

SUNDAY NIGHT Mary wanted to go hear some live music at Muddy Creek, which is a little café in Bethania. Peter Asher, from the old 60's group Peter & Gordon, was playing. He was probably most famous for being the brother of Jane Asher, who Paul McCartney dated several years in the mid 60's. The concert was good—it surprised me—and it also gave me time to reflect without having to talk too much with Mary. During the first intermission Mary asked me if I was okay—I don't know what made her ask that question—but I lied to her and said I was fine. I was not fine...I was still in shock.

I had never given the thought of dating Ida even the remotest of chances. I mean...she was Ida! Ida from Panera, Ida who gets me peanut butter and makes coffee. Not anyone I would date. That's why all the angel sightings and predictions from Joel never made any sense to me. Why would I ever date Ida? Plus, I was dating Mary. Well, I imagine not really dating in the truest of definitions. I don't know what it's called we're doing, but I like it and I want it to continue. But, I have to admit, Ida did look pretty good.

I knew Mary had to get up early Monday morning so I took her home after the concert. Again, she gave me a nice, long hug and once more asked me if I was alright. After a long hug from Mary, I'm always alright. I can't imagine how I'd feel if she ever kissed me. Will she ever kiss me? That is the question.

Monday morning I have a decision to make: I can go to the old Panera and endure a peanut butter-less bagel, or I can go to Ida's

Panera and have peanut butter. I think I'll go to the old one. I truly, honestly have no idea what I would say to Ida if I saw her this morning. I decide to get a cinnamon crunch bagel with my coffee—maybe I can endure it if it has enough cinnamon on it.

As the young girl hands me my tray and I turn around, I see a woman walking toward the door that looks exactly like the mystery woman who spoke to me that day in line, saying, "She's not right for you." Before I can decide whether to say something or not, she's out the door. But as she opens the door, a slip of paper falls from her coat or purse or something. It floats to the floor and I quickly set my tray down and walk over to pick it up. It's a plain piece of unlined paper with these words handwritten on it: "Do the right thing, Jerry."

I quickly walk out the door, looking left and right, but she's gone. Where? I don't know, but she's gone. I stand there a minute or two hoping I might see her drive by in a car, but I don't. I put the slip of paper in my pocket and walk back in the store only to find that a clean-up person has dumped my bagel in the trash can. Great!

"Do the right thing, Jerry." I swear, if Joel happens to show up, I might just punch him in the nose, or better yet, knock out a few of those shiny, straight, white teeth!

After work, I drive downtown to the sidebar at H&H for a drink and a talk with my cousin, Joe. I like these late afternoon times before it starts getting busy with the professional drinkers. When I walk in I see Joe and a customer having a heated (I think) discussion about something. From my perspective the guy Joe's talking with is a twenty-something yuppie. His hair is a little long and his arm has a tattoo of a piece of barbed wire on it. Very original. I walk to the far end of the bar just as this guy and Joe are ending their conversation.

I can tell Joe is a little upset as he walks over to me. The yuppie guy gets up and walks past us towards the bathroom. When he's gone, Joe says, "Jerk!"

"What happened?" I ask him. Joe doesn't immediately answer; he just shakes his head. Then he snarls, "Politically correct? That's just a term used by jerks like him which means 'whiney, overly-sensitive pansies who need everything sugar-coated.' Sorry, Jerry, I don't mean to talk about your friend like that, but I'd really like to kick his butt. Comes in here and orders a craft beer I've never heard of, then complains we don't have it and says we shouldn't be prejudiced against minority brewers. I hope he drowns in the toilet!"

When I'm sure Joe's finished ranting, I ask him, "What do you mean 'my friend,' I've never seen that guy before."

Joe stops wiping the bar, looks at me, and replies, "He said he was waiting on you."

"He said he was waiting on me? Did he say my name?"

Joe explains, "Yeah, he ordered this idiotic craft beer that I've never heard of and said he was waiting to meet his friend—you. He said your full name: Jerry McRacken."

"Joe, I've never seen that guy before in my life!"

"Well, he knew your name, and it seemed like he was expecting you. Did you tell anyone you were coming over here?"

I thought for a second. "No, I just decided after work to drive over. I never even spoke to anyone."

Joe says, "Well, if he hasn't drowned in the can, we'll figure it out when he comes back."

But he never came back. We waited and waited—he never came out. There is a back door, but it's locked. Joe checked it and the deadbolt is still locked from the inside. The guy was not in the bathroom, or the women's bathroom (we checked, just in case). He didn't go out the back door and he didn't come back past us. I asked Joe, "Did he say what his name was?"

"No. I didn't ask him. He only said he was waiting on you."

I thought this sort of weirdness had stopped. I didn't know what else to say, then I thought, "You said he ordered a craft beer you've never heard of. Do you remember what it was?"

Joe nods and said, "Yeah, I remember because it was so weird...Angel's Delight."

Other customers started filtering in the bar and Joe became busy, hopefully forgetting about this weirdness. I did not forget. I got a beer and went to a corner table to think. If this guy, or being, or whatever he was, was indeed waiting on me, then why did he leave? What did he want with me? And, how did he know my name?

Two beers later and I still had no answers to my questions. A group of young guys came in the bar and started getting loud and boisterous, the way young guys do when they're all trying to impress each other, so I had to leave. I walked down the street to my new, beautiful Saab and there he is—the dude from the bar is standing next to my car. I slowed a bit, just to make sure it was indeed the same guy, but I knew it was.

When I stopped, he said, "Hi, Jerry."

It was then that I noticed there was no tattoo of barbed wire on his arm.

"Who are you?"

He grinned a little and said, "A friend."

I was not grinning when I replied, "You're no friend of mine."

He continued grinning and said, "Jerry, you'd be surprised how many friends you have."

"What do you want?"

"Jerry, we just want to make sure you make the right choices in life."

I wish I could've slapped that grin off his smirky, yuppie face. Instead, I asked, "What choices are you referring to?" As if I didn't already know.

"Who you're spending your time with, Jerry. You need to really think about your future and do the right thing."

I still wanted to slap him...hard! Before I could think of anything else to say, he turned and moved away from my car to a bicycle leaning against the building. He hopped on, but before he started to pedal away, he turned to me and said, "Joel says hello."

29

MARY IS FIGHTING a little cold, so I haven't been to her house since Sunday. Tuesday I went back to the old Panera...but it's not the same. Today, I make the drive over to Ida's Panera. Not to see Ida! Just Ida's Panera. They have everything I'm lusting for—not Ida! I'm minding my own business, enjoying the morning and having a second cup of dark roast coffee. And out of the kitchen comes Ida.

She walks to my table and without asking sits down opposite me. She's changed a little. Even though she's still wearing the prerequisite Panera costume, she looks different. She definitely has on makeup, and somehow her shirt is more tailored to her body. Maybe it's just because I've seen her differently, out of the costume, or maybe...I don't know. But she's different. She says, "Jerry, we need to talk."

"Okay. What do you want to talk about, Ida?"

"You know full well what we need to talk about."

I do know what we need to talk about, but I think it's in my best interest not to know at this point in time. So I fake ignorance, "No, I don't. What is it that's bothering you, Ida?"

She shakes her head a little and says, "Jerry, you don't get the same moment twice in life. We had our moment and it didn't work out. I'm okay with that and I wanted you to know that I don't expect you to call me, or even want you to call me. We're not right for each other, Jerry—plain and simple."

Was I being turned down before I even asked her out? Not that I was ever going to ask her out, by the way. Not knowing exactly how to respond to this, again, I faked ignorance and said, "What do you mean?"

"Jerry, we're completely different, you know that. Different everything. You went to college; I only went to Forsyth Tech for a couple of years. I'm a Christian and you, I think, are not. I live in the country—and like it—but you're a city boy. I really don't like dressing up, whereas you are always dressed up. I'm not a drinker, but I'm pretty sure you are. And Jerry, what is this obsession you have with peanut butter? Can you explain that?"

I could answer each of these comments individually and try to refute them or explain them. But, why? They're all the truth. Or I could tell her that an angel came down from heaven and ordered me to marry her and have a baby girl. Then raise that girl and watch her get married and have a baby girl of her own—by which time I'll be dead, by the way. Then wait for our granddaughter to move out west, get a job with the Park Service, and save a man's life. Then marry that man and wait for him to discover a cure for pancreatic cancer. Yeah...I could tell her all that!

However, somehow, I get the feeling she'd probably stop me at ". . . an angel came down from heaven . . ."

So, I take the cowardly, spineless, and wimpy alternative and just say, "Okay, Ida. Goodbye." And I get up to leave Panera for the last time.

I was hoping Ida would stop me. I was hoping she'd say something...anything! But she said nothing. I went to my car, started the engine, listened to the perfectly tuned engine whir to life, and I cried.

"Why? Because I know we won't have a granddaughter together? No. Because Joel will be disappointed in me for not following his instructions? No. Then why, Jerry?" Shut up, little voice in my head...you'd never understand.

By the weekend, Mary was feeling better and we had a busy time planned. She wanted to go canoeing on the Yadkin River Saturday and then cookout at her house Saturday night. I thought canoeing would be fun and easy. It was not fun and it was not easy; and because we wore life jackets, my view of Mary was irreparably hindered.

I thought we'd sort of float along with the current...wrong! We paddled constantly. If not, the current would take us from one bank to the other and crash us against some trees or rocks. It was a struggle I was not prepared for. When we finally completed our journey, we were both exhausted. My only solace being that when Mary took off her life jacket, she had nothing on but a thoroughly wet tee shirt.

Ever since Mary and her girlfriend broke up, she's been braless—even though she told me she would start wearing one. Is this a subtle hint? Keep dreaming, boy. She's just more comfortable not wearing one. I know that, but it's still fun to dream.

We go back to Mary's house for our cookout and she tells me to get things started while she takes a shower. It's pretty simple actually; all I do is turn on the propane gas and let the flames start up. Mary has some hamburgers in the refrigerator, so I take them out and set them on the table. On second look, I don't think they're hamburgers at all. Are you kidding me? Are we going to eat "garden burgers"?

As I'm contemplating this unfortunate turn of events, Mary calls out to me from the bathroom, "Jerry, are you out there?"

"Yeah, what's up?"

"I forgot to bring a towel in here. Can you get one out of the hall closet for me?"

Huh? Does this mean old Mary is naked and alone in the shower? Does this mean she really wants me to bring her a towel into the shower? When she's naked and alone? What does this mean? No...I'm reading too much into this. I'll get the towel and she'll crack the door open and I'll hand her the towel through the little crack in the door. Idiot!

I find a towel in the hall closet and, as I'm about to knock on the bathroom door, she opens it--all the way. Let me repeat that...she opens the door all the way. She's standing there with nothing on her body except little drops of water. At first, I think it's a huge accident. But when Mary doesn't move, or take the towel from my hands, my mind starts spinning all sorts of nefarious thoughts.

I half way hand her the towel but she doesn't make an effort to take it from me. Instead, she says, "Why don't you shower and I'll get the burgers started." Then she takes the towel from me, but doesn't dry herself with it or use it to cover up with. She just slowly walks out of the bathroom towards her bedroom holding the towel with one hand.

Quick thoughts: Mary has a great butt. Mary has great legs. Mary has great body. Mary is gorgeous. Is this a sign? Does Mary want me to follow her into the bedroom? Quick—think! It's too late; she closes the bedroom door. I get undressed and step into the shower, thinking and hoping that Mary may join me in the shower. That does not happen. Only when I get out of the shower do I realize I don't have any clean clothes to put on, only the dirty ones I've been sweating in all day. At that moment the bathroom door opens and Mary is now standing there, fully clothed, with a towel in her hand, looking at me standing there dripping water and totally naked.

I wanted to check my manhood to see if the shower had diminished its presence, but I couldn't take my eyes off Mary's eyes. Then I noticed Mary's gaze start going downward. Fortunately, I felt my manhood react to the situation in a positive way. After a moment or two, Mary handed me the towel and turned around to walk away, without speaking a word. I didn't notice it initially, but with the towel she handed me was also an old pair of unisex gym shorts and tee shirt. They were both large and baggy, but the gym shorts were totally inadequate in attempting to disguise the excitement within.

We had our cookout and ate garden burgers. We nibbled at a salad (at least Mary did), and we both enjoyed our baked potatoes. Mary had some sort of fruit salad for dessert, which surprised me by being very tasty. Not as tasty as Mary would've been right out of that shower...but I digress. We did not mention either shower incident, mine or hers. It was as though neither one happened. After we cleaned everything up, Mary invited me to come to church with her in the morning.

Again, I'm confused. Is she asking me to spend the night and go to church with her in the morning? Or, just go to church with her in the morning? Life is getting too hard. I find out quickly when she says, "Be careful driving home. I'll come by your house in the morning and pick you up for church. Okay?"

"Yeah, great. Thanks for a fantastic day, Mary." And I truly meant it! She hugged me as usual, and I'm quite certain that my baggy gym shorts failed to suppress the stimulation created by that lasting hug, which was now firmly pressed against Mary's body.

I had dreams of Mary. They were not dreams of us in church. They were not dreams of us paddling a canoe down the Yadkin River or of eating garden burgers. They were good dreams...as all dreams should be.

Mary picked me up for church Sunday morning wearing an old pair of baggy blue jeans and a faded blouse (with a bra this time). I had on a coat and tie and was a bit stunned by the way she was dressed. "Aren't we going to church?" I asked.

"Of course we are. Get in."

At this point I guess she understood my concern and said, "You're fine, some people dress a little casual—that's all." Well, when she said, ". . . some people dress a little casual . . ." what she really meant was that EVERYONE dressed a little casual, except for yours truly. I was in a time warp, as though I was living in the 1950's (and dressed accordingly) and had been transported into the 21st century still wearing my 1950's clothes.

Since when did people start wearing blue jeans and shorts and tee shirts and flip flops to church? I did not get that memo! Then, when we were seated, and every eye was on the coat and tie wearing new guy, a rock band started playing. Well, not rock & roll music, but not Amazing Grace either. Two guitar players, a bass player, an organist (not pipe organ), and a drummer started playing and people started clapping along. Some of them even set their Starbucks coffee cups down and stood up and started swaying to the music. It was almost like Woodstock transplanted into Winston-Salem—minus the drugs and sex and good music.

Eventually the preacher got things calmed down. Will, the preacher, was wearing blue jeans and sandals, but he did have on a collared golf shirt. Aside from the music, the rest of the service was fairly normal and reverent, except when the band played another song and several children went up front and started dancing. When it all ended, nearly everyone in the church came up to me and Mary and invited me back next week. I felt very welcome, though totally out of place. Mary seemed unconcerned and happy to be with me. And even with all the non-conformity, I was indeed happy to be with her.

30

WELL, UNFORTUNATELY, the whole Ida issue is now settled. My next dilemma is figuring out the relationship between Mary and me. After the nude, shower scene, things were, more or less, normal between us for a couple of weeks. We'd have dinners, go to movies, and hang out, doing all the things normal "friends" would do with each other. That was the issue..."friends."

I am unsure if our relationship is evolving into something more, or if it's stuck eternally in the friendship mode. And I know this sounds totally weird, but I'm not completely and totally convinced that Mary is...well, let me avoid that subject for the time being. The only thing I am sure of is that whatever relationship Joel was hoping for between me and Ida is not going to happen. I have not been back to her Panera and I have no intention of going back there.

I had told Mary that my old Panera bakery quit stocking peanut butter, and how much I was disappointed by that, when one night she surprised me. She handed me a shopping bag with three boxes in it, all the same thing. I took one out and it was a package of eight separate, one serving cups of peanut butter. I couldn't believe it! I now had my own peanut butter I could easily carry into Panera to use on my bagels. That Mary is a good old girl.

I told her I was taking us out to dinner to celebrate my good fortune and she said, "Okay, just give me a minute to jump in the shower." I instantly forgot what year it was, what my dog's name is, or even if I have a dog. But nothing happened. She didn't call for me to bring her a towel and she didn't stand there naked looking at me. She didn't do anything except take a shower, change clothes, and say, "Okay, I'm ready."

We had a nice dinner at Mama Zoe's. Mary had a vegetable plate of green beans, steamed broccoli, and a side salad with a glass of water. I had the pork chops, pinto beans, mashed potatoes with gravy, and sweet tea. I also had pecan pie for dessert. Mary had no dessert but she did taste my pecan pie. I took her back home afterwards and we ended the evening with the obligatory long, very comforting hug. Which I loved. But, let's face it...I want more. The question is: Will there ever be anything more?

The little servings of peanut butter Mary bought me are perfect. I can now go to my old Panera, get my choice of bagel and hot coffee and have my peanut butter with no worries whatsoever...until HE shows up. It's been so long now, I was hoping he'd forgotten about me—but no. As soon as I set my tray down and say a little prayer (Mary's influence on me seems to be working), Joel is standing right in front of me. "Mind if I join you, Jerry?"

He's not dressed like a hobo today. He's clean shaven again and dressed as though he was on his way to work somewhere. I look up at him and reply, "Yes, I do mind." He ignores me and sits down anyway. I am not going to let his appearance ruin my first day of peanut butter, so I start buttering everything up and then take a bite before I look at him.

He starts smiling and says, "You really like peanut butter, don't you?"

"What do you want, Joel? I tried it with Ida and it didn't work out. I knew it wouldn't. Why don't you go interfere with someone else's life for a change?"

"You didn't try very hard, did you, Jerry?"

"Look, I don't know who or what you really are, but let me tell you something about us earthlings...when a woman says 'don't call me,' then you don't call her! If you do, that's called stalking or harassment. Maybe they didn't teach you that in hobo school."

He continues smiling at me, as though he was even amused at my last statement. Then he gets up, knocks on the table twice, and says, "Try harder."

"Let it go boy. Don't let him get to you. What makes him think he can tell you what to do?" For once, I'm tending to agree with the little voice in my head. Why would I listen to a hobo anyway? And, if he's not a hobo, then what is he? Aren't angels supposed to be nice and help people? I remember Oprah used to have a TV show about angels and they were always "good" people—never like Joel! I think I'll have a second cup of coffee—dark roast!

Mary has some sort of church meeting tonight so I'm left alone. I'm thinking about going downtown to see my favorite bartender, Joe, when the phone rings. I answer, "Hello."

"Jerry, it's so good to hear your voice again. How've you been?"

It takes me about three or four seconds for her voice to register, but there's no mistaking Danelle.

"Danelle, wow, I didn't think I'd be hearing from you again. Are you married yet?"

A moment of silence, then she answers, "No, not married. Not to him anyway. We broke up, so I'm sort of free again."

I know I shouldn't have said anything, but it just came out anyway, "I never thought for a second that you were not free."

"I guess you're right, Jerry." Then another moment of silence before she continues, "I was wondering what you're doing tonight? Maybe you want to get together."

I remember last week's sermon was on temptation. Is this karma or what? First, I have someone who might be an angel trying to influence me. Now I have the devil himself trying to lure me back into the depths of carnal intrigue. Mary would never know if I succumbed. No one would know if I fell into this temptation. I could unleash my pent-up sexual urges and satisfy my cravings while temporarily quelling the desires of another human being. There's only one problem: I would know.

"I can't, Danelle. I hope things work out for you, I truly do. But I can't. Bye, Danelle." That being said, I hang up the phone before any demonic urges rise to the surface and change my feeble, little mind.

My bartender cousin, Joe, has called me a few times wondering why I haven't been down to see him. But I've been so busy with Mary, I simply haven't had time. Wednesday night, Mary was going to a Bible study that didn't end until 8:00 and then we were going to get something light to eat (light in her case, not in mine). So, I decided I'd drop by Joe's place for a couple of hours before I met Mary. It was a fairly slow night which allowed us to have some uninterrupted time to talk.

"Where the devil have you been?" He says. Funny he uses that word, when I'm absolutely certain Mr. Lucifer himself is exactly the one who tempted me with Danelle earlier.

"Just been busy. You know how it is." What can I tell him? I'm not "dating" anyone—exactly. He'd never understand my relationship Mary or why I'm spending so much time with her, so I continued my lie: "Work's been tough and I just got tied up with stuff, nothing in particular."

Joe, nodding his head, then says, "It's the gay girl isn't it?"

"No! It's not the gay girl, and I'm not even certain she is gay."

He stops nodding and tilts his head at me and asks, "You think you can turn her, don't you?"

"Turn her? What are you talking about?"

"You're thinking if you just hang around with her, be her friend, let her see how cool you are and what she's missing, that she'll change her entire personality and want to hook up with you. I can see it in your eyes, Jerry. You're so transparent, you're almost invisible!"

"You're crazy, Joe! Where does this wild stuff come from? Mary and I are just friends—nothing more, nothing less. And I haven't seen her that much anyway." Why do I always have to lie?

I can tell he doesn't believe anything I'm saying. Then he asks, "What happened with Danelle? You had a good thing going with her? How'd you screw that up?"

"I didn't screw anything up, Mr. Know-It-All! She was getting married!"

That stopped Joe dead in his tracks. He said, "Married?"

"Yeah, she was engaged to this older guy and was going to marry him."

Joe took a few seconds to digest this new piece of information, then said, "I find that very hard to believe, numbskull."

"And why is that?" I asked, rather smugly.

"Because after she dumped your sorry little butt, I moved in with her!"

I heard that sentence very clearly, but I simply couldn't comprehend the meaning of it. Joe has moved in with Danelle?

She just called me trying to get me to come see her! I didn't know what to say. No reason for me not to believe him. No reason for me to believe Danelle wouldn't indeed do exactly what it seems as though she has done. I was still silent when a guy at the bar waves at Joe because he wants a drink. Joe starts towards him and looks back at me and said, "Your loss, my gain."

I picked up Mary after her Bible study and asked where she wanted to go. She said, "I'm not really hungry, are you? Let's just go to H&H and have a glass of wine."

Well, first of all, I'm very hungry. Second, H&H is where Joe works. Third, Mary never drinks wine. And fourth, there ain't no way in the world I'm going back there tonight and face Joe!

Fifteen minutes later we walk in H&H and Joe waves at us. The place has filled in and I don't see any open tables anywhere. Joe waves us over to him where there is one open bar stool next to an older guy slumped over the bar next to his drink. We walk over and Joe says gleefully, "Hey, Jerry. Long time, no see." Then he taps the guy on the head who is slumped over, and says, "Alright, DL, that's enough. Time for you to go home."

Poor old DL shakes his head, looks over at Joe, and says, "Yeah, okay, thanks. See you tomorrow, Scott." And he gets up and stumbles towards the door.

I take the now vacant stool and ask Joe, "Who's Scott?"

Joe answers, "I have no idea and neither does he. How are you doing tonight, Mary?"

She looks at me, then back at Joe, and says, "I didn't know you knew my name."

Joe smiles and replies, "Oh, yeah. Jerry's told me all about you. What can I get you to drink? It's on the house!"

Mary smiles, saying, "That is so nice. Just a glass of white wine, please."

When he walks away, she looks over at me and asks, "So, what did you tell him?"

"I haven't told him anything! He's lying. He's a bartender. You can't believe anything he says."

Mary sits there nodding at me, knowing I just lied to her, but she's too nice to call me on the lie, so she only says, "Okay, whatever you say."

Joe comes back and sits a glass of wine in front of Mary. He hasn't brought me anything. He says, "So I hear you two have been dating quite a while now...anything serious?"

Do you know how loud bars are at night when they are fully packed? Right. H&H was fully packed when Joe said that but I didn't hear anything—nothing at all—except the sound of sweat popping out on my forehead. Trouble was coming, I knew it was coming, and I didn't know how to avert it. How can I explain this? I'm going to kill Joe! Mary's expression never changes. She takes a small sip of wine, then looks back at Joe and says, "I wouldn't really call it dating, Joe. It's better described as unadulterated, uninhibited, extreme sexual fantasies involving two or more consenting adults on a regular basis." Then she looks at me and says, "Isn't that pretty accurate, Honey?"

I hope she is not expecting an answer from me...because I have none.

Mary's comment actually shuts Joe up. He walks away without a word, and he never brings me anything to drink, or returns to us. Mary pushes her glass of wine over to me and I drink it in silence. We sit there, staring at nothing, and when the noise becomes too loud and the silence becomes too deafening, we go back out to my car. When I start the engine, Mary says, "Well, that certainly was interesting."

"Mary, I . . ."

But she put her hand up and says, "Not tonight, Jerry, let's just go home."

We ride in silence until we got to her house. Before she opens the car door, still looking straight ahead, she says, "Don't worry about anything Joe said. I know he's full of it. But I do need to think, Jerry. I need to know how I feel and what I want. It's something I have to figure out. Okay?"

And before I could answer or respond in any way, she opens the door and says, "Call me tomorrow sometime."

31

I DID CALL MARY the next day, but she told me she needed a "few days" to think about things. That was two weeks ago. I went to church alone each Sunday hoping to see Mary, but she was never there. One day, after the service, I asked the preacher, Will, if he'd heard from Mary, and he said, "I really can't discuss those things with you, Jerry. I hope you understand."

Yeah, great! You'll discuss angel sightings with me, but you won't talk about the girl I'm in...what, Jerry? What are you in?

Work has become boring for me. I don't know if it's because I've been doing the same thing for a long time, or if the money has simply made it unnecessary for me to work any longer. At any rate, I'm seriously thinking of...umm, not retiring--I'm too young for that...but finding something I truly want to do, something that would be fun. I'm in the positon that money would not be the primary factor in a new job. Rather, it would be doing what I love to do—what I want to do. My little voice suddenly perks up and says, "Okay, Jerry. Tell me what it is you DO want to do. Just tell me what you DO love doing." Dang you little voice in my head! Why can't I have a job eating bagels and drinking coffee?

I go to Panera every day to eat and think. I'm halfway successful. I almost wish Joel would show up and tell me something...well, almost. This morning when I finish my coffee and walk outside I see Mary, of all people, standing next to my car. She waits on me to arrive and has this ominous look on her face that concerns me a bit. I stop in front of her and say, "Hey...are you okay?"

"I think I am, Jerry, but I'm not a hundred percent sure. I want to tell you something that probably won't make sense to you. It didn't make sense to me at first, but now I think it does."

"Okay, Mary. Tell me. Or would you rather wait until tonight when you're off work?"

She takes a half step closer to me and says, "No, I need to tell you now. Then, tonight we can talk about it after you've had time to think."

I start to say something, but she stops me and says, "Let me finish...Jerry, there's two things I'm sure of, which don't make sense. First, I'm certain I'm gay."

Hearing that absolutely drains my enthusiasm for the moment.

"Second," she continues, "I'm also certain that I need you in my life. I've been asking myself if a gay woman can actually be attracted to a man, and still be gay? I've never been attracted to any man before—never. But when I'm with you, I don't want to be with anyone else. Does this make sense? I want to be with you, even though I know I'm still gay—and it feels right to me."

I wish she'd keep talking, because I truly do not know how to respond. All I do know is that I also want to be with her. She keeps looking at me, so I finally say, "You're right, it doesn't make a lot of sense initially. But I do know that I want to be with you and I want you to be with me. If we both want the same thing, how can it be bad?"

Mary smiles and replies, "I'm so glad to hear you say that. We can try, can't we, Jerry?"

"Of course we can. I think it'll all be good."

Mary smiles even bigger and gives me a long hug there in the parking lot.

Then she says, "Can you come over tonight?"

"Sure," I say. "Do you want to do something?"

Mary looked up at me and says, "Yes...something."

Mary went back to work. I tried to go back to work but was unable to concentrate, so I feigned sickness and went home. I'm certain the "something" Mary alluded to is the same "something" I've been hoping for months on end.

When I got home I tried to take a nap, but after twenty minutes of fidgeting, I gave that up. Then I tried to read, but words were no solace to me today. Maybe if I ran around the block a few times I'd burn off some of this excitement and nervous tension I have built up. I made it around the block fine the first time. The second time was bit of a struggle. I stopped half way around the third trip, and started walking. Running is harder than it looks.

Anyway, two and half trips around the block was enough; that's probably what...six or seven miles? I turned the last corner in the direction of my house and I see an old man with a cane walking towards me. He's not actually using the cane to help him walk; he's actually sort of twirling it around, while he's whistling. I've stopped running, but I'm trying to impress the older gentleman with my "power walk" as I come near him. When I'm a step in front of him, he stops whistling and looks at me and says, "I just love this song, don't you?"

Being polite, I stop beside him and say, "I didn't really hear it. Do you mean the one you were whistling?"

"Yes. It's great isn't it?"

And he starts whistling it again. I nod, but actually have no idea what song it is. I'm thinking early onset of dementia. So, to placate him, I reply, "Yes, sir. It's very nice."

He stops whistling and says, "You don't recognize it do you?"

Time for honesty, "No, sir, not really. It sounds familiar, but I can't place it."

He says, "It's by George Strait. Do you know him?"

Well, yes, I know who George Strait is, but I certainly don't know any of his songs. So I tell the old guy, "Yeah, George Strait...which song is it?" I'm hoping this will terminate our little dialogue and send the old man on his way.

He stops twirling his cane and looks me dead in the eye and says, "It's called 'Do the Right Thing,' Jerry." And just as suddenly, he starts twirling his cane and whistling again as he walks away.

I'm taking my shower before going over to Mary's house, trying not to think about that old man. I'm not going to let anything ruin this evening. I don't really care what songs George Strait sings, or what any of them mean. And, I AM going to do the right thing—hopefully, several times. I only hope that I haven't misinterpreted Mary's meaning of "something." Something to her could mean "we go out to dinner" or "we go to a movie" or "we cook out garden burgers" or even "we sit around, drink bottled water and discuss our feelings."

"Something" to me has quite the different connotation. These things weigh on my mind as I'm driving over to her house. When she opens the front door and I see each room lit only by candle light, and I hear a CD of Joni Mitchel playing, I think we're pretty much on the same "something" page. Mary is wearing something flowing--I'm not sure what it's called--but I'm pretty sure there's nothing on underneath it. When I walk in the door she hands me a glass of wine, Riesling I think, but at this point in time I'd drink motor oil if Mary handed it to me.

She picks up her own glass from the table and says, "I hope you don't mind, but I've already started." I'm hoping she's referring to the wine and not something else I was dreaming of. She spills a little wine on the floor and says, "You're not hungry are you?"

"No, the wine and you are all I need."

She smiles at my romantic inference and says, "Make yourself comfortable, I'll be right back."

As she walks, a little awkwardly, back to her bedroom, I drink my wine as quickly as I can, hoping to get near the same level of nirvana Mary has already achieved. She comes back after a minute or two and her wine glass in empty. She sees mine is now empty as well, so she asks, "Do you want more wine...or, maybe something else?"

I quickly rise from the couch and say, "Something else! Definitely something else."

She reaches out for my hand and leads me back to her bedroom, where she has lit several candles all around the bed and nightstands. The bed covers have been turned back and Mary stops at the edge of the bed and turns to face me. Then she takes her left hand and uncovers her right shoulder and allows the gown she's wearing to drop to the floor. She definitely has nothing else on. Then she takes one step towards me and says, "Kiss me, Jerry."

After all this time, after all my dreams...finally, my wish has come true. I kiss Mary and put my hands around her body, allowing one hand to edge down around her butt. Then, as we're probing each other's mouth and lips, I start thinking to myself, "I have my hand on Mary's butt. Mary's naked body is pressing against my chest. This is MARY I'm kissing!" Then something happens. I pull back and look in her eyes at the exact same moment Mary vomits all over the front of my shirt.

After the vomiting stops, Mary's eyes close as she collapses on the bed, unconscious and blithely oblivious of the moment, from too much wine, I'm assuming. Her breathing is normal and she's making slight humming noises. I cover her up and go into the bathroom to try and clean my shirt off. No point, it's ruined. I remember once, when we did something together, Mary wore an old men's shirt that buttoned up the front. I open her closet and rummage around until I find the shirt. I put it on; it smells like Mary but fits fine. Then, I go back to the bed to make sure she's still breathing okay, which she is—in fact, she's started snoring. I go to a chair in the corner and sit and think and wonder...what in the world just happened?

Okay, let me analyze this: a beautiful woman takes her gown off in front of me. Then she asks me to kiss her. We kiss. And suddenly, I have the overwhelming feeling as though I'm kissing my third grade teacher! Or worse—my sister—and I don't even have a sister! All this time of lusting for Mary and then when I have my hand on her butt, it felt as though I had my hand on Lucifer's chopping block and he was getting ready to cut it off.

Maybe Mary won't remember any of this when she wakes up. Maybe things will be different the next time. Next time? No, no, no...there will be no next time. I can't go through this again! How am I ever going to explain this to Mary? I go to the refrigerator to get a glass of wine to help me relax and think. There's only a little left in the bottle, so I pour what's left in my glass and rinse out the bottle to put it in Mary's recycle container under the sink. When I do, I see two other empty wine bottles already in the recycle container. I instantly think, "The city just picked up recycling yesterday." Mary, oh Mary...did it take two and a half bottles of wine for you to convince yourself to kiss me?

Mary didn't wake up all night. I dozed and thought and dozed some more in the chair beside her bed. As the first rays of morning sun begin to filter through the curtains, I notice Mary begin to move around a bit--not opening her eyes, but changing positions from one side to the other. After about fifteen minutes of this, she yawns and stretches her arms over her head. Then she sits up in bed, sees me staring back at her and screams. "Jerry!! What are you doing here?" But before I can answer, she asks, "What happened?"

I'm not really sure she's asking me or asking herself this question.

Next, she grabs her head and says, "My head's killing me." She flops back on to the bed holding her head and asks me to go into the bathroom and bring her some Excedrin and water. When I bring it to her, she quickly realizes she's not wearing any clothes and the bed sheets are down around her waist. She fumbles around trying to cover herself up, but the sheets are a tangled mess. She ultimately gives up and takes the water and pills from me saying, "I don't care." I tug at the covers and unravel them, then cover her up while she's still holding her head.

I don't know what to say, or even how to start saying anything, so I sit back down in the chair and wait. After a few minutes, she looks over at me and asks, "Isn't that my shirt?"

"Yeah, I borrowed it. Can I bring you anything else?"

Her eyes move around a little, and there is a slight frown on her face, and she asks me, "Did anything happen?"

"Aside from you getting drunk, puking on me, and passing out...no, it was a pretty normal night."

"Oh, Jerry, I'm so sorry. I was just...I was...I'm sorry, Jerry. I just can't do it. I love you, but not like that. Do you hate me?"

"No, I could never hate you. I love you too, Mary, and I know exactly how you feel. Even if you hadn't puked all over me, I couldn't have done anything. It just didn't feel right. Like it or not, we're friends and only friends—stuck with other in a bond of weird, serendipitous friendship."

Mary smiles and says, "Come here and give me a hug, then go home and let me sleep. And, I want my shirt back!"

32

ODDLY ENOUGH, the following week Mary and I fell back into our older, more comfortable relationship—being only friends. It was easier on both of us now that we understood the dynamics between us. One evening I'm sitting around home—alone— listening to an old Doobie's record, "What Were Once Vices Are Now Habits," and the futility of my personal life fully dawns on me.

First, I break off my imminent marriage to Jennifer, which made me very happy and probably hurt Jennifer's financial plans more than anything else. Then my mom dies rather unexpectedly. I meet Danelle, who takes me places I've never been before, in a mostly impersonal, physical way. Then just when I think I've found what I'm looking for with Mary, I learn that things aren't always what they seem to be. So, here I am, back to square one, wondering what in the world is in store for me. Will I ever find the woman who is right for me? Will Joel's predictions come true? (I honestly doubt that one.) Or, will I continue my disheartening odyssey for true love through on-line dating services and bar scenes?

I have now been back to Panera for over three weeks, since Mary and I had our personal revelations, and I haven't glimpsed any angelic or supernatural behavior. I'm getting a little lonely. The coffee is still good, the bagels are fresh and tasty, the peanut butter soothes me, but something is missing...I miss talking to Ida. I never really "talked" to her per se, but it was comforting knowing she was there to take care of me—in a Panera sort of way. Then, we had that one meeting, when I saw Ida as she truly was, not as I had always assumed her to be. I can't forget how she held my hand that day—it was reassuring and heartening. And, I really can't forget her legs as she walked out of TJ's Deli that afternoon. I never dreamed Ida could look like that. What have I been missing?

I begin to consider the thoughts that maybe I should visit the Panera across town, where Ida is, just to see if there is even a scintilla of interest on her part from the result of our meeting. I know she told me not to call her, but did she really mean it? After several cups of dark roast coffee, I finally convince myself that she did indeed NOT mean it. I know Ida wants me to see her again...even Joel wants me to—I think.

The next morning, I make the drive down Stratford Road, through all the mall traffic, past the putt-putt place, past the myriad of restaurants and shops, and make the right hand turn at Village Tavern, almost running over a guy in the road selling newspapers. I'm high on adrenaline as I walk into Panera, rehearsing the things I'll say to Ida when I see her. They're busy today; four people are in line in front of me. All the staff are scurrying around trying to get things done.

I see the Hispanic assistant manager, who looks at me then turns away without speaking. Then, I see a middle-aged guy come out from the kitchen with a "Manager" label on his shirt. Do they have two managers here? Has Ida transferred again? What's going on? I'm next in line and the young lady asks if she can help me and I say, "Yes, is Ida here today?"

"Ida? What is that?"

"It's not a what," I say, "It's a who. She's the manager. Is she here today?"

The young lady seems totally perplexed by this line of questioning and calls over a goofy looking nerdish guy and asks him if he knows anyone named Ida.

He says, "Yeah, she used to work here, but she left."

I looked back at his eyebrow-pierced eyes and asked, "Are you sure?"

"Well, yeah, dude. She left."

This is hard for me to accept. I ask him further, "Do you know where she went? A different Panera?"

"I don't think so, dude, but you can ask William. He's the manager. He might know."

I move to the side, out of the line, and wait for William to come around again. When he comes out of the kitchen I wave to him, hoping to catch his attention. I think he thought I had a complaint about something, and he walks over with a very professional look on his face and says, "I'm William Coleman, the manager. What seems to be the problem, sir?"

"Sorry to bother you, William. There's no problem. I am just trying to find my friend Ida and was hoping you could tell me what happened. Is she not here anymore?"

William nods and says, "I can't really go into that, but I can tell you that Ida does not work here any longer—her choice."

"What happened?"

"I can't go into that, sir. I hope you understand. Is there anything else I can do for you?"

I can't believe what I'm hearing. "Did she leave a number to get in touch with her?"

William is getting a little irritated with me now and says, "Sir, you know I can't give out any personal information. Ida's not an employee here and there's really nothing else I can tell you. Okay?"

"Okay . . ." But it really isn't okay. Ida is gone and I don't know where. Why did she leave? Where did she go? And where the devil is Joel when I actually need him?

I logged back into the dating site, but Ida had removed all her information and wasn't in their directory at all. I wanted to discuss this with Mary but somehow it just didn't feel appropriate, especially now since Mary had gotten another letter from ex-girlfriend asking about the chance of a reconciliation. She would be coming home from her tour of duty in Afghanistan and wanted to see Mary to try to work things out. I hope they're successful.

Mary and I had a few garden burger cookouts and vegetarian pizza nights, but I could tell she was preoccupied with thoughts of Teri, her ex-girlfriend. I'm a lost and lonely soul. Time to visit my cousin Joe.

When I walk in the bar, Joe is at the far end and yells out to me, "Where's your gay over-sexed girlfriend?" On second thought, I turn around, walk out, and go down the street to Foothills Brewing, a local craft beer pub. They have outside seating at Foothills so I find the only unoccupied table and take a seat. I order a Pilot Mountain Pale Ale and sit and watch the traffic pass aimlessly by—reminding me of my life in a figurative sort of way. I think I'll have one more, then take my sorry, lonely self back home and watch a MLS game tonight on TV...that's how far into the depths of despair I've fallen.

When the waitress comes back to take my order, I'm temporarily distracted by the lack of tattoos on this young lady and not actually paying attention to what she says. I assume she is asking me if want another beer, so I answer, "Yes, and that'll be all, thanks."

In fact, that's not at all what she had asked me. She replies, "Okay, I'll bring you one, but I was asking if you minded if someone sat here with you? We're all full inside."

"Oh...I'm sorry; sure, no problem, tell him to come on out." She smiles, goes back in, and shortly comes back with a woman who has orange hair, tattoos on both arms, and piercings in her ears, nose and lips. Well, this is going to be fun. The woman, and I honestly cannot tell if she's young or not young, sits down and offers her hand to me saying, "My name's Marianne. Thanks for sharing the table with me."

I shake her hand--she has a very firm handshake for a woman--and say, "I always liked the name Marianne, ever since Marianne . . ." But before I could finish, she says, "Marianne Faithfull, yeah, I know. She dated Mick Jagger—did you know that?"

Well, no, I didn't know that. And I wasn't thinking of her; I was thinking of my eighth grade teacher, Marianne Hudgins. But I guess I'll take the easy way out of this awkward introduction and just say, "No, I didn't know that."

Marianne orders a Carolina Blonde from the waitress as we inspect each other without further comment. My plan is to drink my Pilot Mountain Pale Ale as quickly as possible and leave Marianne to her faithfulness. The silence between us is fairly uncomfortable, so I try to ease the situation a little, and ask, "Are you originally from Winston-Salem, Marianne?"

"No."

"Do you work here in town?"

"No."

I wish I'd ordered a shot instead of a beer so I could down it in one gulp and be gone. The waitress brings the Carolina Blonde back to our table, but Marianne doesn't touch it. She just continues to stare a hole through me. Okay, one more sip, to be polite, and I'm outta here. As I pick up my glass, Marianne leans forward in her seat and says, "You know she's waiting for you, don't you?"

I looked around just to make sure she wasn't talking to someone else—she wasn't. Quite dumbly, I ask, "What?"

"You heard me quite clearly, Jerry. Don't blow it."

And with that, Marianne stands up, without ever touching her beer, and walks back inside Foothills. Yeah, I heard her clearly enough. But what did it mean? Who's waiting for me? It's too late for me and Mary—that's done! I'm NOT calling Danelle again. Or Jennifer. And I don't know how to call Ida.

I'm not going to let this rest; this Marianne girl is going to explain herself! I walk inside the pub and it is indeed crowded, but, as you probably already know, there is no Marianne. I find my waitress and ask her if she's seen the tattooed girl anywhere. "No, I thought she was sitting out with you."

"Did she pay you for her beer?"

The waitress has this worried look on her face, and replies, "No, she said you'd be paying."

Well, my supernatural occurrences are now taking on a new financial twist. I walk through the pub looking around, then I wait outside the women's restroom, but I know...trust me, I know. She will not appear again.

33

MARY'S GIRLFRIEND, Teri, finally came home from her tour in Afghanistan with the Army, and she and Mary are a couple again. Good for them, bad for me. I've been spending so much time with Mary that I've forgotten how to be on my own. From what I understand, Joe and Danelle are quite the couple now. No comment. And I heard through the grapevine that my ex-fiancée, Jennifer, has found her a lawyer and is very happy. I received a wedding invitation from Jennifer's attractive friend, Casey, but decided not to attend the ceremony—better all around.

I've gotten to the point at work where I'm not happy any longer. I don't know if the money I inherited has jaded me or if I'm simply bored, but I need a change. The only thing I've done with the money is to buy the new Saab. I even went shopping one day at the dreaded mall and must've stopped and looked in over fifty stores but never bought a thing.

I turned in a two-week notice at work. I'm not sure what I want to do; I'm only certain that I don't want to be doing this any longer. I'll figure something out. Maybe I'll travel some. I've always wanted to visit Canada and maybe Alaska—I heard it's pretty up there. I haven't seen or heard from my old nemesis, Joel, in quite a while. I hope he's not too mad at me because things didn't turn out like he wanted them to.

Friday was my last day at work and they gave me a little going away party. Everyone kept telling me how lucky I am. I wish I could believe them. The only good thing recently has been that I had fallen into the regular habit of attending church every week.

My old preacher friend, Will, is a good speaker and even though I can tell he wants to ask me about any "sightings" I've had, he doesn't.

I went to visit a travel agent to explore options and was talked into a "single's cruise" in the Caribbean. The agent told me there'd by hundreds of available women on the cruise and it should be a blast. Sitting in the travel agency, it all sounded great. Now that I'm supposed to leave, however, I'm a little anxious about it. I'm really not the mingling, talkative type guy who can start up conversations with strange women. I like comfortable. Sometimes, I can really act disgustingly old.

I need to be at the airport in Greensboro Monday morning at 11:00 to catch a flight to Miami where I'll board the cruise ship. Joe has volunteered to tear himself away from Danelle long enough to drive me over there so I don't have to leave my car in the long-term parking lot. As he drops me off in front of the terminal, we both unload my luggage and he hands me a pack of condoms and says, "Make sure you put these to good use."

Good old Joe...always looking out for me. I put the package of condoms in my pocket quickly before anyone else can see them. I'll probably throw them away when I enter the terminal. Joe drives away and I feel a lonely sense of despair. I'm tempted to wave a taxi over and go back home. I probably would if I knew Joe wouldn't find out-- I'd never hear the end of it. So I trudge forward, checking my bags, then through security, where I have to empty my pockets and let everyone around me see all the condoms—thanks, Joe.

I continue down the walkway to Gate 37 where my flight will be leaving in about an hour and a half. There's a coffee shop near that also sells pastries, so I get a scone and a cup of over-priced coffee and settle down to wait for my flight. I'm hoping the connecting flight isn't late because I'm already nervous about this entire ordeal. In a few minutes I see the plane taxing up to our gate. When all these people leave, then we can board and I'm on my way—hopefully, before I change my mind.

I throw my half full cup of coffee away and get in the already forming line as we wait for all the other passengers to exit. I know a lot of people love travelling, but from the looks on the faces of all the people leaving this flight, it doesn't seem as if anyone is having fun. They all look tired, worn, and frustrated. Old men and women, hipsters, young kids, and...IDA????

Is that Ida? Of course it is, idiot. What is she doing exiting this airplane? Quick—THINK! Do I half turn away and try to avoid her? No, numbskull! Before I can stop my mind from racing and come to a conclusion, she walks right up to me, stops, and says, "Jerry, I can't believe it. I never thought it would be true."

I don't know what to say or how to respond to that. But before I have to, Ida continues, "But here you are. You ARE waiting for me. I didn't believe him."

I have about a hundred questions, but which one to ask first? "Believe who, Ida?"

"Joel. He told me you'd be here waiting on me. Remember him? Jerry...he's not a hobo. You won't believe what I think he is."

My mind is still racing as I'm trying to organize this information in my head. So, to confirm what I've just heard, I ask her, "Joel told you I'd be here?"

"Yes. I was visiting my parents in Phoenix and had planned on staying several more days, but I was out shopping one day and saw Joel standing in front of a Barnes & Noble Bookstore. I couldn't believe it! He waved to me and I went over and we started talking. He said he was meeting someone and had to leave, but told me—no, ordered me--to change my plans and be on this flight. He said you'd be here waiting for me. Obviously, I thought he was crazy, but I didn't tell him that.

217

"Then he moved to stand directly in front of me and peered straight into my eyes, Jerry. It was weird. Then he repeated his orders to change my plans and be on this flight. I think he could tell I didn't believe him, so he put his hand on my shoulder and said, 'Ida, just so you'll know I'm serious and that you should believe me, I'm going to tell you something.' And, Jerry, you'll never believe what he told me about the future, our future: kids, grandchildren, all sorts of crazy stuff.

"When he told me this fantastic story, Jerry, I almost started laughing in his face, it was crazy. Then, he said, 'Ida, look at me. Look directly at my face, then close your eyes for one second— ONE SECOND ONLY.'

"I did that, Jerry. I stood not two feet from him, I could smell his breath, then I closed my eyes for ONE SECOND, and when I opened my eyes...he was gone! He was gone, Jerry. After I stopped trembling, I went back to my parent's house and changed my flight--and here I am."

I am totally incapable of speech right now. But looking into Ida's eyes and seeing her face gives me the most comfortable feeling I've ever had in my life. Then Ida starts again, "I know this is hard to fathom, Jerry. But why else would you be here to meet me? We're like two rivers merging together. Joel spoke to you and told you to be here as well, didn't he?"

Now would probably not be a good time for me to tell the truth. So, I tell a partial truth, "Yes, I have spoken with Joel. But still, Ida, do you believe him? Do you believe this fantastic story? Do you believe in me?"

Ida steps closer to me and says, "Yes, Jerry. It's always been you. I just never thought you ever paid any attention to me before. I knew it was you the first time you ever walked in Panera...I just didn't know how or when."

✤

Ida and I gathered her luggage and went outside to call a taxi. I figured I'd call the airlines and have them send my luggage back from Miami--she doesn't need to know about that. She also thought it was very romantic that I had taken a cab over to the airport so we could hold hands in the back of the cab on the way home--I'm so thoughtful.

We hopped in the back of the taxi, holding hands and more excited than I can ever remember being. As I shut the door I happened to notice a well-dressed black man, with graying hair, standing at the curb smiling at me with the straightest, whitest teeth I've ever seen.

The End

Afterword

A GOOD LIFE is when you assume nothing, do more, need less, smile often, dream big, laugh a lot, and realize how blessed you are.

Okay, okay...I'm getting there. Larry, thanks again. All my misplaced dots and commas appreciate your hard work. I owe you a beer or two—not at "Crafted" however.

www.ingramcontent.com/pod-product-compliance
Lightning Source LLC
Chambersburg PA
CBHW060918180626
46817CB00004B/1307